An UNEXPECTED Legacy

An Unexpected Legacy

AMY R. ANGUISH

Tulpen Publishing

An Unexpected Legacy
Tulpen Publishing
www.tulpenpublishing.com

© 2017 Amy Anguish
Cover Design by Roseanna White
http://www.roseannawhitedesigns.com

All rights reserved.

No part of this publication may be reproduced or transmitted for commercial purposes, except for brief quotations in printed or electronic reviews, without written permission of the author or publisher.

An Unexpected Legacy is a work of fiction. Names, characters, places, and incidents are either a product of the author's imagination or are used fictitiously. Any resemblance to actual persons, living or dead, events, or locales is entirely coincidental.

Printed in the United States of America.

ISBN: 978-0-9962746-2-3

Dedication

*For my daddy, the man who has always
encouraged me to do my best, believed I could
do anything even when I doubted,
and been my biggest fan.*

I love you.

Prologue

~1978~

"Don't even think about it."
Sandy stared across the room at Rob's eyes. Spellbinding. The brightest shade of blue she had ever seen. "About what?"
Ruth stepped between Sandy and her view. "That boy."
"Which one?" Sandy asked, although she had a guess. She trailed her finger along the snack table, reached for a pretzel as a way to get a better view. His new letterman jacket hung loosely on his lean frame, his long fingers playing with the edge of his Bible as he stood talking to several other boys in the youth group.
Ruth turned Sandy to look at her. "You know which one. That Manning boy. That family's no good."
"How can you say that?"

Ruth huffed. "Are you coming or not?" She motioned toward the door. "Daddy's waiting in the car."

Sandy intentionally walked around the table in the opposite direction of her older sister so she could get a little closer to Rob as she left. Her heart sped up a bit as she wondered what it would feel like to have her hand in place of his Bible. He looked up, noticed her stare, and gave her a grin before she could duck her head.

Ruth caught up and nudged Sandy again as she slowed down. "Do you know where they're living?"

"In the old Potter house." Sandy frowned. "What does that have to do with anything?"

Ruth opened her mouth, as if to say something, then shook her head. "Just leave him alone, Sandy. He's no good for you. You're going to end up with your heart broken."

"Don't be silly, Ruthie." Sandy pushed the door open. "I'm going to marry that boy."

Chapter One

~2011~

Jessica Garcia sat on the patio of Smoothie Heaven, a Christian romance on the table in front of her. The scent of honeysuckle hung thick in the early fall air from the vines growing up the trellises that blocked the patio from the parking lot. Normally, this time of year in central Texas was still too hot to really enjoy the patio, but a rain shower had come through earlier in the afternoon and a nice breeze ruffled her hair and the pages of her book. As Jessica took a long slurp of her chocolate smoothie, she believed this had to be the perfect way to start a weekend, even one she had to work.

Laughter from one of the other tables made her look up. Three women and two men were audibly having a great time. The group had disturbed her peace the whole time she had been there. Her gaze lingered on the taller man.

His long, tapered fingers bent a straw paper and straightened it out again and again. She always had been attracted to hands. His blue eyes weren't hard to like, either. He was the one making everyone laugh as he regaled them with some story about a dog. The three women at his table couldn't take their eyes off of him. He glanced Jessica's way and she promptly looked back to the page in front of her.

Propping her cheek in her hand, she tried to hide the heat that burned her skin. The words which once completely held her interest now had no appeal whatsoever. She made it halfway down the page before giving up and admitting she hadn't paid attention to anything she'd just read. She willed herself to not look up to see if those blue eyes were still looking her way. He had no reason to watch her—like she had been watching him—but was he?

"You look really familiar," a deep voice said as she returned to the top of the page for the third time in a row.

The eyes she had admired from several feet away were even more gorgeous up close, not just one shade of blue, but layer upon layer that sparkled like a sapphire. "Wh ... what?"

"I said you look familiar." He cocked an eyebrow. "Have we met?"

"I don't think so." She made an obvious attempt at reading her novel, despite the fact that she hadn't turned a page in the last ten minutes.

He pulled the chair around in front of her and straddled it. "You're sure?"

She slowly moved her book to just below her line of sight. "I can't remember ever meeting you before."

"Chad Manning." He held out his hand.

She studied his outstretched fingers, long and inviting. Finally, lowering her book, she shook his hand. "Jessica Garcia." Yes. Those fingers were warm and appealing.

"It's nice to meet you, Jessica." He held on for just a moment longer than necessary ... and she found she couldn't complain.

A cough from the other table drew her attention. She was suddenly aware that his friends were all quietly watching their exchange. He followed her gaze over his shoulder and they all motioned for him to come back.

"Guess I'll have to hope you come here a lot so I can bump into you again." He slowly rose from his chair.

"I do," she replied before she could stop herself.

He grinned and tipped his cup toward her. "Then so will I." With that, he sauntered back over to the other table.

Jessica gave herself a little pinch to make sure a scene from her book hadn't come to life. Nope. He was really over there stealing glances at her over his shoulder, while the women tried to regain his attention with an exaggerated flip of blonde hair over a shoulder, a loud giggle, scooting their chairs closer to him, a touch to his arm. Jessica put her bookmark in place and walked to her car before she did something crazy like slip him her phone number. Maybe owning a bookstore wasn't good for someone like her—she saw heroes all over the place, even when she didn't know anything about them.

***

"Wait. He said what?" Courtney Pennock, Jessica's best friend, roommate and half-owner of The Book Nook, sat in the overstuffed chair in their living room, cross-legged, while Jessica filled her in on her smoothie adventure.

"He said 'Then so will I.'" Jessica tossed a strand of choppy brown hair out of her face.

Courtney raised her eyebrows. "Sounds sort of stalker-ish."

"No it doesn't!" Jessica leaned closer and shook her head.

She and Courtney had been best friends all four years of college, roommates for most of those, and had owned The Book Nook for the last three. Even though they were really close, they were almost complete opposites. Courtney, in Jessica's mind, was the prettier one with her long hair and blue eyes. Jessica was the one more tuned to romance, though. Her mama called her eye color gray, but she tried not to let her eyes turn envy-green when looking at her roomie.

"I still say it's weird that he just came up to you out of nowhere and started talking to you." Courtney unfolded her lengthy legs from the chair. "Besides, I thought you said you weren't ready for another relationship."

"I'm not." Jessica followed Courtney to the kitchen. "I was just telling you what happened." Jessica only came up to Courtney's shoulder, and she had to force herself not to walk on tiptoes around her tall roommate.

"Which is why you can remember how long his fingers were and how blue his eyes were." Courtney batted her eyelashes.

Jessica bumped her roommate out of the way to get a mug down. "You're just jealous something so romantic didn't happen to you."

"Says the girl not interested in romance right now." Courtney bumped Jessica back.

"Have I told you lately you're hard to live with?"

"No. Tell me." Courtney grinned.

"You're hard to live with." Jessica made a silly face.

"I hear we Texans usually are."

Courtney was the reason Jessica had ended up in Texas. She had no family close to her in the Austin suburb of Honey Springs, but Courtney had convinced her to move down here anyway to help her run a used bookstore. They had gotten a better-than-great deal on the building because of Courtney's parents' realty business. The old house had previously been converted into a furniture store with the living quarters upstairs. The prior owners had agreed to leave all the bookshelves when they moved out. With the kitchen already on the second floor, the girls didn't have to do a lot of work when they moved in.

"I still can't believe you moved me down here. My sister thinks I'm a lost cause." Jessica took a sip of coffee.

"That's because she's a die-hard Oklahoma fan, and she can't stand that Texas wins all the time." Courtney wiggled her eyebrows.

"Or something."

"I still think you should get her that bumper sticker as a joke for Christmas." Courtney leaned against the counter.

"Remind me what it says."

"I wasn't born in Texas, but I got here as soon as I could." Courtney laughed.

"She'd never forgive me." Jessica sat at the table and flipped through the mail.

Courtney gave a theatrical gasp. "What if the guy from the smoothie shop is from Texas and you end up marrying him? You might be stuck here forever!"

"Oh, please." Jessica waved her hand in the air as if to swat away a pesky fly. "I already told you. It was just a fluke. I'll probably never see him again."

"But what if you do?" Courtney leaned in closer.

"I probably won't."

"Just like you don't really want another relationship."

"I don't." Jessica looked up at her friend. "Not yet. Austin ... Austin scarred me a bit. I'm not sure I can risk that again."

"I know, Jess. I'm sorry." Courtney sat at the table with her. "We get anything good in the mail?"

"A couple bills and this catalog for all those clothes you like so much."

"Sweet!"

Jessica was glad that Courtney had willingly changed the subject. Austin Vasquez was still a bad road to go down. And being teased about wanting a new relationship was too close to talking about Austin. The girls flipped through the clothing catalog and then agreed to call it a night.

Jessica shut the door to her room and grabbed her romance book to read another chapter or two before she turned out the lights. When she opened to where she had been reading at the smoothie shop earlier, she found a business card tucked in the pages with her bookmark. The name Chad Manning made her heart skip a beat. The outline of a dog and cat took up most of the front with a veterinary clinic name, and his cell phone number scribbled at the bottom.

Jessica twirled the card back and forth in her hand. How'd he sneak it between the pages without her even noticing? She turned it over but the back was blank. He obviously wanted her to call him or he wouldn't have gone to such lengths to give her his number. She carefully tucked it further back in her book. There was no way she would actually call him. But it would be good to have the contact information in case she ever got a pet ... or something.

"I'll probably never see him again," she whispered to herself.

Chapter Two

"Hey girls." Jessica slipped into her normal seat in Bible class Sunday morning between Mary and Amber. They both shot several glances at the doorway. "What's caught your attention?"

"Mm. Just wondering who the new guy is." Mary nodded toward where people were coming into the classroom. "He's quite dreamy."

Jessica glanced up to see a familiar set of baby blues staring back at her. She hoped her eyes weren't really as wide as they felt. Chad Manning walked into the room with the same guy he had been with at the smoothie shop and sat on the other side of the room.

"Earth to Jessica." Amber waved her hand back and forth in front of Jessica's face. "You still with us?"

Jessica blinked and swallowed. "Yes."

"Didn't look like it." Mary smirked. "I saw him first."

Jessica grinned back. "Actually, I met him Friday night. But don't worry. I'm not in the market for anyone right now, so he's still fair game."

"Sounds good to me." Amber straightened in her chair, rearranging her blouse as she cast a glance at the other side of the room.

When Courtney and Jessica started worshipping at Northside church of Christ, they had gone to a class called The Mingles. It was supposed to be a mix of Singles and Young Marrieds. Since then, the congregation had grown and the class had been split in two: Young Professionals and Young Marrieds. The girls, both single, went to the first one, taking turns teaching second grade on alternating quarters. This month, Courtney was in charge of the elementary kids and Jessica got to sit in this class. Half of her wished she had been teaching this morning instead of sitting in the same room as Chad Manning.

"I have just a few announcements." Rich, their teacher, cleared his throat, interrupting any further discussion by standing behind the podium and starting class.

Jessica settled her Bible on her lap. She could feel Chad's gaze boring down on her, but she refused to meet his stare. She kept her focus on Rich as he continued to talk.

"Every year the Williams family invites our class out to their ranch for a hayride and bonfire devotional." Rich paused as several people murmured their excitement. "This year it's going to be October fifteenth. We're having it early so that it won't conflict with the kids' Trunk-or-Treat on the thirtieth." He pointed to a clipboard near the back of the room. "There's a sign-up sheet being passed around as well as directions on how to get there. I think this year they're actually talking about doing the haunted hayride down where all the people jump out at you—not just around the ranch. Should be fun. Everyone come."

Jessica wrote the information across the top of her bulletin and then put Courtney's name on the list with hers. She knew her roomie would want to go again this year, especially if they were really going to do the haunted ride. Jessica wasn't much into stuff like that, but Courtney was the kind of girl who could watch horror films all day long.

As class got under way, Jessica stole a glance to her left and studied Chad from her peripheral vision. He wore a Polo and khakis. The aquamarine blue of his shirt made his eyes even brighter than they had been a few days before. He looked her way, and she returned her attention to the chapter in Genesis they were discussing. She blinked, trying to focus on the words in her lap and what was being said. How could she be so distracted? She hardly ever struggled to pay attention in class.

Rich was reading from the story of Joseph. "'Thus he left all that he had in Joseph's hand, and he did not know what he had except for the bread which he ate. Now Joseph was handsome in form and appearance.'"

I wonder if Joseph's eyes were like the blue of the ocean ... like Chad's eyes. Jessica caught the direction her thoughts were heading and mentally gave herself a shake. This was ridiculous! After fighting through several more mental meanderings of the same sort, class was finally over and she scurried to meet up with Courtney for worship service.

"How were the second graders?" she asked her roommate.

Courtney hugged the packet of next week's lesson to her chest as they maneuvered through the crowd to their usual section on the front right side of the auditorium. "Brody gave me a little trouble, but Seth recited all his books of the Bible today. Just two more kids and we owe them an ice-cream party."

"Yay." Jessica couldn't help but smile. She and Courtney had decided at the beginning of the school year to challenge the kids to learn all sixty-six books by promising ice cream. They had no idea it would only take them a couple months to actually do it.

"What'd I miss in class?"

"The Williams' hayride and bonfire is on the fifteenth. I signed you up with me since I knew you'd want to go."

"Of course." Courtney gave a thumb's up.

They slid into the pew with Amber, Mary, Garrett, and Sam.

"And they're talking about doing that haunted hayride, too." Jessica nudged her friend.

"Sweet." Courtney pulled a card out of the back of the pew in front of them to mark down their attendance for the week.

"Jessica, did you tell her about the handsome stranger?" Mary leaned over Amber to ask.

"Handsome stranger?" Courtney raised a brow at her roommate.

Jessica scowled. "Remember how I said I'd never see that guy again? The one from Smoothie Heaven?"

"He's here?" Courtney looked around as if she could spot him, despite not knowing what he looked like.

"Yes. He came in with the same guy he was with the other day, and they sat on the other side of the room during class." Jessica shrugged. "That's all I know."

"So, where is he now?" Courtney scanned the auditorium.

"Don't know." Jessica focused on filling out her attendance card. "He's not my responsibility."

"That's not very Christian-like. You should have gone up and welcomed him and everything, since you already met him." Courtney poked her in the shoulder.

"How did you meet him, Jess?" Amber asked, her long brown hair hanging like a perfect curtain as she leaned over.

"He randomly introduced himself to me at the smoothie shop the other day." Jessica hoped she wouldn't have to give more details than that.

"Mind if I sit here?" Chad stood at the end of their pew, talking with Garrett and Sam.

"You didn't tell me he was so tall," Courtney whispered.

Jessica elbowed her in the side.

"What?" Courtney's teasing voice belied the innocent look she wore.

Jessica didn't bother to answer. She instead chose to ignore the fact that everyone had bunched up closer to her to make room for the man who had been in her thoughts for two days now. She was used to being squished a bit on this pew—not many of the Young Professionals wanted to scoot back to start a second one so they were always squeezing another one in. She placed her Bible in her lap as the service started. Nothing was different than normal and if she kept pretending that, maybe it would become true.

"Are you giving God everything you can?" Gregory Pikes, the preacher, asked from the pulpit half an hour later. "Or are you more like the one-talent guy? The guy who was so afraid to use what he had been given that he hid it away for fear of losing it."

Jessica mentally scolded herself. She honestly couldn't recall most of what the rest of the sermon had been about, but that question about whether she was giving God everything was obviously not true. What was wrong with her today? She had spent so much energy concentrating on facing the front and not glancing to the right during the worship service that she ended up with a crick in her neck.

At the end, she snatched up her Bible and purse, ready to make a dash for the doors, only to discover that she was trapped in the middle of the row. Courtney, Amber, and Mary were chatting to her left. To her right, the boys were discussing the coming deer season. She plopped back down on the pew to wait.

Why was she in such a hurry to get out? Why did she want to avoid meeting Chad again? It upset her to know that the other girls found him attractive, though she wasn't sure why. She traced the letters of her name on the front of her Bible as she waited for Courtney to finish talking.

"I guess you're waiting on me, huh?" Courtney finally looked down at Jessica sitting there.

Jessica shrugged. "You are my ride." They usually took turns driving to church and this was Courtney's week.

"Fancy meeting you here." Chad leaned over the pew in front of her.

Jessica slowly lifted her head to meet the most startling blue eyes she had ever seen—bright and dark at the same time, as if she were looking into the depths of the ocean—staring right at her.

"It's Jessica, right?" From his towering stance, he grinned down at her.

She nodded. "And you're ... Chad, right?" She would never tell him she'd been taking his business card out, looking at it and putting it back in her book over and over again for the last twenty-four hours.

"Right." Chad gave a thumb's up, not taking his gaze off of her. His friend nudged him, and Chad abruptly faced him. "And this is Brian. He's new in the area. I talked him into going to church with me, but he didn't seem to like where I was going, so I agreed to go with him here this morning."

"Where do you usually go?" Courtney asked.

"This is my roommate, Courtney." Jessica motioned toward her friend.

"Nice to meet you." Chad shook Courtney's hand. "I usually go down to a congregation in Round Rock, but Brian decided it was too big. He's a small-town boy."

"We were just about to go to lunch." Amber leaned around Courtney. "I'm Amber, by the way. Why don't you join us?"

Jessica tried not to glare at Amber. Her attempt to keep them together longer was absolutely unnecessary. Why did Jessica want to get away from this dangerously handsome man? Did she want to get away from him? She needed time to sort this out. Flirting with someone at a smoothie shop when you didn't think you'd ever see him again was one thing. Running into him at worship services, a place she frequented even more than Smoothie Heaven, made him a bit more real. And she wasn't ready for real yet. Was she?

"Can't today." Chad pointed at his friend. "Brian has to be at work at one. Maybe another time?"

"Man, you guys should come to the hayride." Garrett slapped his shoulder.

"Maybe I will." Chad's gaze flickered to Jessica. "If I don't see you before then, it was nice seeing you again, Jessica." He turned to everyone else. "Nice to meet you all."

***

"What is wrong with you?" Courtney's long legs ate up the short distance to the car and Jessica had to walk faster than normal to keep up.

"Nothing." Jessica straightened to her full height.

"Something's wrong with you if you're not interested in such a nice and dreamy man, Jessica Garcia. He is hot. You better get down to the smoothie shop every day and hope you run into him again."

"Courtney Pennock, you are nuts." Jessica slammed the door with more force than necessary. She didn't dare admit that she had already thought about hitting up Smoothie

Heaven to see if she could run into him again—although, maybe not for another week or two. She definitely didn't need to rush into anything despite what her roommate thought.

Chapter Three

Jessica didn't have a chance to speak with Chad again before the night of the hayride. She had no idea if he would show up but she ran a brush through her hair an extra time just in case. Then she shook her head at herself and pulled on a hat. Courtney didn't mention anything as they drove down the county road past cow pastures and random convenience stores to the ranch. Jessica fidgeted with the air vents, then with her package of hot dog buns, then with the foil on Courtney's rice cereal treats.

"Will you please just admit you're interested in him?" Courtney put her hand on top of Jessica's to keep the foil from rattling.

"I don't know—"

"I know you've looked at his business card so many times the ink is wearing off. I know you saw him at church the other night and couldn't help yourself from looking his way half the service. I know you scribbled his name on the back of the receipt book and then marked it out thinking I wouldn't realize what it was. Why not just go for it and see where it leads?"

Jessica fixed her gaze on the central Texas landscape outside her window.

"He's not Austin, Jess. You're never going to get over this fear of getting your heart broken until you go out there and try again." Courtney gave her hand a squeeze as they pulled into the gate of the ranch. Prickly pears bordered the metal fence, and the oak trees shed their leaves as they drove down the driveway to where everyone parked on the grass.

Courtney was right. Jessica just wasn't sure how to convince her heart.

They walked up to the ranch house where everyone gathered in the backyard around a stack of wood that would be the bonfire later. They placed their food on the tables and went to join their friends next to the big trailer hooked up to Randy Williams' pickup truck. Hay bales lined it, and blankets were scattered around for when the night got cooler. Bonnie Williams brought out a huge Crock Pot full of chili, and Randy had about fifty hot dogs going on his grill. The air was crisp, but not cold. Perfect bonfire weather.

"Is your boyfriend coming, Jessica?" Sam asked as she and Courtney joined the group. He leaned his long frame against a metal lawn chair and Jessica wondered how it didn't fall over.

"Boyfriend?" Jessica cocked an eyebrow.

"The guy who was at church the last couple of times, brown hair, blue eyes, tall. You know." Garrett nudged her. He had become the little brother Jessica never wanted.

"I don't have a boyfriend." Jessica brushed his hand away from her shoulder like a pesky fly. "But if you're asking if Chad will be here, I have no idea."

"I would say, yes." Mary pointed. "Here he comes now."

Jessica couldn't help herself. Her eyes followed the direction of Mary's finger to where Chad walked toward them. He wore jeans and a flannel shirt and carried a couple of sodas. He smiled at her and before she could help it, she smiled back.

"Are we eating first?" He joined them, standing between the guys and Jessica.

Amber sidled a bit closer.

Garrett pointed to the tables. "We'll eat hot dogs and chips first—then hayride—then bonfire with marshmallows and s'mores." He shrugged with a grin. "Personally, I just came for the food, but I've been informed I have to go on the hayride, too."

"You'd better." Mary elbowed him. "Otherwise, who am I going to sit by?"

Garrett looked around their group. "I don't know, Mary. Any one of these fine people?"

Garrett and Mary had been friendlier with each other for a while now, but were still denying that they were actually a couple. Jessica suspected they would be official soon. She had seen them holding hands during the prayer at church earlier in the week.

"I'm going to go see if Bonnie needs any help in the kitchen." Jessica quickly stepped away from the group. This was a public setting and perfectly safe for her to test the waters with Chad. She just needed to work up to it. And the electricity between Garrett and Mary only added to her desire to charge into something similar with the handsome veterinarian.

"Hey, Jessica. What are you doing inside?" Bonnie looked up from emptying a bag of chips into a bowl.

"Just wanted to see if I could help."

"Sure." The older woman gave her a smile. "Grab that bag of cheese and carry it outside, would you?"

Jessica set off across the yard with the cheese and several utensils. Her eyes scanned the group of friends still talking near the trailer, but Chad wasn't with them. With her focus fixed elsewhere, her foot snagged on a root. The ground rose up to meet her, and her knee hit the dirt.

Chad caught her by the elbow, as well as several forks. "You okay?"

Where did he come from? She tried to catch her breath as well as hide her embarrassment. "Fine. Just clumsy."

He helped her straighten. "I'm glad you didn't get hurt."

"I even saved the cheese." She held up the bag and then berated herself mentally for making such a stupid statement.

"Hot dogs are ready!" Randy called from the grill as he forked the last one onto a large aluminum tray.

Jessica had never been so grateful for processed meat. "I better go put this on the table."

Everyone gathered in a big circle and Sam led them in prayer, thanking God that they could be together for a good time and for the food. Then everyone loaded paper plates with chili dogs and chips and sat around in lawn chairs to eat and laugh. Chad ended up across the circle from Jessica, and she kept stealing glances at him between mouthfuls of hot dog and chatting with the girls. Several latecomers straggled in and ate quickly so everyone could go on the hayride. Around fifteen climbed aboard the old farm trailer.

Jessica decided to sit at the front and Courtney sat to her right. They perched on the hay bales and pulled a blanket over their legs as everyone else piled on.

Chad strode up and pointed to the spot to the left of Jessica. "This seat taken?"

She shook her head and he sat next to her, the scent of his shampoo wafting over her as the breeze blew her way. He leaned back against the railing and his arm brushed against hers.

"So, what all is involved in a haunted hayride?"

Courtney leaned forward. "I think there're guys with chainsaws and silly masks that jump out and try to scare you as you ride through this park they've got decorated with tombstones and stuff." She waved her hands in the air as she described everything, almost knocking Jessica's hat off. "It's silly, but fun."

"Chainsaws?" He raised his brows.

"They've taken the chains off. It's more for the noise-factor. To make you feel like you're in a horror film or something." Courtney laughed. "I love it. That's why I organize the mysteries and horror novels, and Jessica is in charge of the romance section."

"Do you work at the library?" Chad gave a confused little frown.

"We own a bookstore together. But it would be all cookbooks and romance novels if it were just Jessica. She doesn't do mysteries or horror." Courtney play-punched Jessica's arm.

"Just not into scary stuff," she gave a little shrug.

"Then why are you here?" He focused his attention on her.

"I like the hayride part, there and back. The ones we went on in college, I would hide behind Courtney when the haunted part was going on. And I wanted to come to the bonfire. There's just something wonderful about singing praises to God with the stars above and the air nice and cool while your front gets toasty from the fire and your back freezes."

"Wow." He laughed. "Doesn't that sound inviting?"

"Okay. So I'm weird." Jessica threw her hands in the air.

"I don't think so." He shook his head, one side of his mouth going up in a half-grin.

She quickly looked away before he could see the blush she knew was creeping up her cheeks.

"Everyone ready?" Randy called out.

All the Young Professionals cheered, and the truck jerked to a start and rolled down the driveway and out onto the county roads.

The cool night air made Jessica glad for her fleece jacket. She tucked several strands of hair back under her hat to keep them from blowing in her face. It was several miles to the haunted park, but the group around Jessica stayed fairly quiet. Several people down at the other end of the trailer grew boisterous; their laughter and jokes carried above the crunch of the wheels and the engine of the truck. Courtney spoke in hushed tones with Amber. Mary and Garrett sat on the left side of Chad and held hands.

The truck slowed and made a right turn into the park. Fake spider webs hung in the bushes on either side of the entrance, and a man in a lab coat and crazy hair jumped up onto the trailer. Jessica shifted a bit in her seat. She really did hate stuff like this, but despaired being a party-pooper.

"Just wanted to give you guys a heads-up as to what's about to happen." Lab-coat guy's voice was rough and gravelly. "This is a haunted trail you're about to embark on. This close to Halloween, the ghosts and goblins come out to play. There might be monsters and murderers, vampires, or any other ghoulish creature you can think of. I have no control over them, so if they decide to join your ride, well, enter at your own risk!"

Several of the guys laughed.

"Watch out for any weapons they might use. Chainsaws might not have a chain on them, but they can still burn you. Don't touch the creatures and they shouldn't hurt you ... much!" The man rubbed his hands together, let out a creepy laugh and jumped off the trailer.

Randy inched forward, and Jessica held her breath.

"You okay?" Chad whispered in her ear, sending a shiver down her shoulder.

"Sort of." She inhaled shakily.

Just then, the first chainsaw started up right next to the trailer, and Jessica jumped, bumping into Chad. He put his arm out to steady her. As the masked creatures crept and pushed closer to their hayride, she snuggled into his arm that remained around her shoulders. A scene set up to the left revealed another man in a lab coat supposedly working on a dead body, fake blood all over the stark white of his costume. To the right, creepilymasked guys leaped out from behind tombstones in a phony graveyard. Jessica knew it wasn't real, but when the guys with chainsaws jumped up on the trailer with them, she closed her eyes and buried her head in Chad's shoulder.

"It's okay," he murmured as he rubbed her arm.

Her friends laughed and shrieked as the chainsaws roared and other creatures moaned and growled. The trailer kept moving forward, and her heart galloped in her chest as one of the machines revved close to her head.

Courtney laughed to her right. Some of the guys taunted the actors as they scared the girls. Chad's arms made a welcome safe haven, and she pushed down the guilty nudge for letting him hold her this way.

After what seemed like an eternity, the last chainsaw died, and silence hung in the air. She slowly lifted her head and looked around to see everyone laughing with one another, several of the other girls also with boys' arms around them. Her hat had fallen off somewhere along the ride and Chad handed it to her. She brushed a strand of hair out of her face and sat up.

Chad studied her.

"I'm sorry about that," she whispered, wishing she could hide under the trailer.

"I'm not." He reached up and gently moved another strand of hair off her cheek. "You okay now? You were shaking pretty good there for a while."

Thankfully, it was dark enough he shouldn't be able to see her blushing. "I'm fine." She straightened her jacket and refused to meet the stare she knew Courtney was giving her. Jessica would never be able to live this one down.

The bonfire blazed soon after the group returned to the ranch. Jessica helped Bonnie lay out metal roasting sticks, marshmallows, chocolate and graham crackers. Several guys grabbed handfuls of marshmallows and a couple sticks each and headed back over to the bonfire to see who could burn theirs the darkest without catching it on fire.

"Do they ever grow up?" Jessica asked Bonnie.

"I hope not." The older woman pointed to her husband who had joined in to poke his stick close to the flames.

The group settled down and the boys led praise songs as the flames danced in the middle of the group. Sparks floated into the sky, a perfectly cloudless expanse where all the stars displayed their glory. Jessica shivered as she and the others praised the God who had made it all. Chad sat next to her, his tenor voice blending with her alto.

Later, as everyone gathered their belongings to head home, Chad pulled Jessica aside. "I enjoyed this evening so much."

Jessica nodded. "I did, too."

"What do you say we get together again next week? See if we enjoy each other even without the rest of these friends?"

"Like a date?"

A corner of his mouth turned up in a grin. "You do date, don't you?"

"I have in the past." She ducked her head.

"It doesn't have to be anything fancy. I just really want to spend more time with you."

Her heart fluttered a little faster. "I'm surprised you'd want to spend more time with a girl who you had to catch earlier as she walked across the yard ... and then who hid her head in your shoulder all through the park." She cast him a sideways glance. "Wouldn't you rather spend time with someone you don't have to rescue?"

He popped the collar of his jacket up and struck a pose. "I don't know. Sometimes a guy likes to be with a girl who needs a hero."

She giggled. "A hero, huh?"

"At least someone with a comfy shoulder." He gave a shrug. "What do you think? Was my shoulder comfy enough for you to want to risk needing it again?"

Yes! her heart yelled. She nibbled her lip a moment before actually vocalizing an answer, though. "That sounds like it might be fun."

They worked out details of where and when to meet before she walked over to join her roommate. She would have to tell Courtney eventually, but not yet. Right now, she simply enjoyed the lingering sweetness of marshmallows and songs next to a very attractive man she hadn't figured out yet.

Chapter Four

Jessica pushed through the glass entryway of Chad's veterinary clinic on Thursday evening. The bells on the door jingled as it shut. The lady at the desk looked up and smiled.

"You must be Jessica. I'll go let Dr. Manning know you're here. He's just finishing up with his last patient."

Jessica perched on one of the chairs lining the waiting room. A big fish tank hummed in the corner, and a dog barked somewhere in the back of the building. She could hear Chad's voice muffled from one of the rooms off the lobby. She tapped her toes on the black and white tiled floor and studied the bright yellow walls. It was definitely a cheery room.

The door opened, and a woman came out with Chad and a huge German shepherd. The dog strained on his leash as if he wanted to greet Jessica, and the woman had to plant her feet to keep him from actually achieving his goal.

"So, just add half a can of green beans to his food in the evenings and that should help with some of his weight issues." Chad handed the dog owner a sheet of instructions. "If it's not working like you want it to, come back and you can try a brand of the weight-loss food. But the green beans are the cheapest way to go for now."

"Thanks so much, Dr. Manning."

Before Jessica knew what was happening, she had a lap full of dog, his tongue licking the side of her face.

"Bruno, no!" Bruno's owner pulled him off and scolded the dog.

Chad helped Jessica to stand. "You okay?"

"Just surprised." Jessica wiped her cheek on the back of her sleeve.

"I'm so sorry!" The owner tugged on the leash. "Bruno just thinks he needs to meet everyone and that they all want a kiss." She yanked again.

"No worries." Jessica held her hand out to the animal and laughed as he pushed his head against her. "Dog slobber is supposed to be clean, right?"

"Come on, Bruno. Let's go put you on a diet." Bruno's owner pulled the dog out the door and the wind slammed it closed.

"I've really got to get maintenance to tighten that so it won't slam so much," Chad muttered. "Well, come on. I'll show you around."

She followed Chad in his white doctor's coat down the blue hallways, while he pointed out the three rooms where he saw his patients. He showed her his office and the office of his nurse, the kitchenette, the bathroom, and then took her to the kennels, where owners could check their pets in for a night or two if they were going out of town.

"There's someone I want you to meet." He grabbed her hand, pulled her into the room on the right, and made a wide sweep with his arm. "The catitat."

"Catitat?"

"You know ... cat habitat. I just shortened it because it sounded better." He winked. "It does sound better, right?"

She grinned. "Very cute."

After slowly opening one of the cages, he reached in and pulled out a little fuzzy bundle of orange and white fur.

Jessica gently accepted it and found two brown eyes looking back at her. The kitten purred as she rubbed his soft head.

"I think he likes you," Chad said.

"Is he yours?" Jessica nuzzled the fur.

"Sort of." Chad leaned against the wall. "One of the girls found him in the alley back behind our building when they were coming in the other day, so she brought him in. He's kind of taken over the place. When we're not taking care of patients, we're back here coddling this little guy. I was thinking he might make a good bookstore cat."

Jessica looked up quickly at that. "I don't know, Chad. Courtney might not like that."

"Is she allergic?"

"No. But since we're co-owners I really should talk it over with her." The kitten tried to climb up Jessica's shirt. She grabbed him by the scruff of the neck and moved him back down again.

"What if I talk to her about it for you?" Chad took the cat out of her hands.

"What makes you think you can talk her into it where I couldn't?" Jessica raised an eyebrow.

"Well, I already persuaded you, didn't I?" He laughed. "One look at this face and who could resist?"

"The cat's face or your face?" Jessica put her hand on her hip.

"Whichever works." He winked. "Want to take him over to meet her?" He wiggled his eyebrows." You know you want to!"

"Chad ..."

"If she doesn't like him, I promise to bring him back and not ask anymore." He crossed his heart with his free hand.

She took the kitten back and looked at it very seriously. "Are you a good mouser? Because I found some evidence the other day and don't want to have to deal with it myself."

Chad laughed. "Come on. Let's go get some kitten chow and a box for you to take him home in."

Jessica followed him back to his office where he draped his coat over his chair and turned off the lamp. He grabbed a bag of cat food, a couple food bowls, and a nifty box that folded into a pet carrier and brought them back to the front desk.

"And how much will I owe for all of this?" Jessica gently set the feline in his temporary cage.

"Give me a kiss and we'll call it even."

Jessica looked up sharply. He raised an eyebrow, and she couldn't tell if he was teasing or serious. She shook her head. "Fresh out of those."

"Hmm. Then, we'll just say that since you're taking the one thing out of the office that's been distracting my whole staff, that we're good anyway." He studied her face. "You're going to save me a lot of time in hunting down the receptionist and nurse."

"Are you sure, Chad?"

"I'm sure." He picked up the box where the kitten meowed and scratched. "Why don't you grab the food and bowls and we'll get out of here."

They walked out into the crisp evening, and he locked the door.

"Is dropping Lester off going to put a kink into whatever plans you had?" Jessica leaned down to peek through one of the holes in the box at the kitten who was mewing pitifully.

"Lester?"

She pointed to the box. "Doesn't he look like a Lester to you?"

Grinning, he shook his head. "No kinks in my plans. I wasn't really sure what we were going to do."

"We could just pick up a pizza and a movie and hang out." Jessica shrugged. "Chilly nights like this I really like to just curl up at home. And I don't want to just drop Lester off and leave him there alone."

"Okay. I'll swing by the pizza place and meet you over there if you'll give me directions."

She followed him out of the parking lot. How was she going to tell Courtney that she agreed to bring home a kitten? It was going to be pretty obvious when she walked in with a bag of kitten chow even if the actual cat was still with Chad. She got off the interstate and drove down Main Street until she got to the two-story Victorian that housed The Book Nook. She had forgotten to tell Chad to park in the back, but he'd figure it out.

Courtney came through the back door as Jessica extricated the bag from the car. "Thought you had a date tonight?"

"We decided to just hang out here and watch a movie," Jessica said.

Courtney looked pointedly at the bag. "We can talk about what that means later. I guess it's a good thing I just made plans with Mary and Amber to have a girls' night out."

"You're not going to be here?" Jessica hadn't been alone with a guy since Austin. Suddenly, the thought of a pizza and movie night didn't sound as good.

"Nope. But I'll be back later. We're just going to go grab a burger and bowl a couple of games."

Jessica nibbled her bottom lip as she glanced up at the house. "Knowing you girls, that could be a while."

"Hey." Courtney held up her hands. "Do you need me to stay? Or come back after the burgers or something?"

"I don't want to ruin your night. This was my idea." Jessica straightened her shoulders.

"Just text me if you need me back early." Courtney hit the button on her key fob and her car unlocked.

Chad pulled into the drive and parked behind Jessica. He got out with the pizza box and the pet carrier and bumped his car door shut with his hip.

"Hey, Courtney. Want some pizza?"

"Can't. Off to meet the girls. You two be good," she said in a sing-song voice as she got into her Honda. "I'll be back when you least expect it."

"Huh." Chad lifted the kitten's box. "So much for showing her the face."

Jessica shook her head. "C'mon in, Chad. I'll hold the door for you."

She showed him around the bookstore briefly before leading him up the back stairs to their apartment. "This place is perfect for us because both bedrooms have their own bathroom. The kitchen is the right size for two. The other room we sort of dubbed the living room or den. We really don't use it much because we're either down in the store or doing something with church."

"Or getting a smoothie."

"Or that." She pulled paper plates down from the cabinet and found some sodas in the refrigerator. He had rented a DVD from the kiosk outside the pizza place and it was on top of the pizza box. They took their dinner, Lester, and the movie into the living room. He didn't act like he thought anything was weird about them being alone together, and she tried to relax. After all, her roommate had threatened to come back at any time. And he had easily accepted it when she didn't give in to his request for a kiss at the clinic earlier. *He's not Austin.*

She took a deep breath to clear her head while Chad opened the box and freed Lester. The kitten sat in the middle of the floor and stared for a minute before tentatively sniffing around and checking things out.

"We can set his litter box up in my bathroom for now." Jessica pointed through the doorway, glad she had made the bed that morning. "You want to do that and show him where it is? Pretty sure Courtney will never forgive me if there's an accident."

"Got it." Chad scooped up the kitten before he could crawl under the couch. She heard him pouring litter as she turned on the television and DVD player.

"What movie did you get?" she called.

"Some cartoon one. I wasn't sure what you were in the mood for."

"I'm always in the mood for animated," she said as he came back in. "Want to pray before we eat?"

They sat on either end of the couch and held hands as he led them in a prayer. Then, she settled on her end of the couch with her pizza in her lap as Lester pounced on a piece of lint between them. Chad looked over at her and then at the cat.

"You're too far away."

She eyed him. "I don't think so."

"Should have gotten a horror film." He grinned.

"Chad ..." She took a deep breath. "I should tell you something."

He paused with his slice of pizza halfway to his open mouth.

"I just got out of a ... well, a complicated relationship. We were together a couple of years, and he thought we should take it to the next level, but what he considered the next level and what I considered the next level were two very different things." She swallowed against the familiar hurt and anger. "When I found out he was ready for moving in together but not marriage, I broke it off, but it wasn't easy. I really thought I loved him."

Chad put down his pizza, but didn't say anything.

"I'm just ... I'm just not ready for anything really serious right now. I agreed to a date, but I'm scared to death." She shifted in her seat. "That's one of the reasons I suggested we come back here. I thought with Courtney in the same building, it might not be so hard ... And then she left, too."

"Hey." He took her hand and leaned forward to look in her face. "It's okay. I'm sorry I wasn't very gentlemanly." He shook his head. "I shouldn't have teased you earlier about the kiss, and I shouldn't have suggested you get any closer to me now. We can go as slow as we need to, but only if you promise me one thing."

"What's that?" she asked softly.

"Give me a chance. Not every guy is like the one you broke up with."

She smiled.

"I won't do anything until you tell me you're ready. And, just for the record, I'd never ask a girl to move in with me before marrying her." He gave her hand a quick squeeze. "Is it okay if I hold your hand during the parts when the witch comes out?"

She laughed and ducked her head. "Yes."

"Oh good." He released a big breath. "I was afraid I was going to have to hide my eyes."

She pushed his arm, and he chuckled before they both settled into their ends of the couch, maybe a few inches closer than they had originally been. The previews flickered to life on the screen, and Lester purred from his position snuggled against the side of her leg.

He's not Austin.

~1978~

"Where ya been?"

Sandy looked up guiltily, having snuck in after curfew. "What are you doing up, Ruthie?"

"Waiting for you." Ruth crossed her arms as she sat on the couch. "You were out with him again. Weren't you?"

Sandy slipped her heels off and hung them from her fingers. "Him who?"

"You know *who*. Rob Manning."

"Yes. I was out with Rob." Sandy couldn't hide the dreamy smile on her face.

"Does Dad know you were out with him?" Ruth stood up.

"Yes. He approves of him." Sandy put her hands on her hips. "You're the only one who doesn't."

"Because you can do better than him."

"I don't even know what that means. He's a great guy, a Christian, and he's smart and funny and handsome." Sandy swayed a little with each adjective.

"You're hopeless." Ruth threw her hands up. "That family is bad news. You need to stay away from them."

Sandy shook her head. "You've said that before, but you refuse to tell me why. Give me the reasons you think their family is so bad. From everything I've seen, they're just as great as Rob is."

"I ... I can't," Ruth stood up and moved as if to head down the hallway. "You're just going to have to believe me."

"Ruthie, what is it?" Sandy frowned.

Ruth paused and looked back over her shoulder. "Sandy, please. Please believe me. He's going to break your heart."

"It's too late to stay away from him." Sandy took her sister's hand. "He's already got my heart. But he won't break it. He loves me, too."

Chapter Five

~2011~

The evening sun cast a golden glow over the trees and bushes around the miniature golf course two days later. Chad stood with his sleeves pushed up and slowly aligned his club with the bright blue ball on the green.

Jessica stood by, tapping her toe impatiently. "Just hit it already." She crossed her arms, feigning impatience.

"This is an important shot." He licked his finger and held it up, as if to check the wind. "If I don't hit it at just the right moment, at just the right angle, the blade of that windmill is going to sweep down and bump into my ball instead of letting it pass through the tunnel to the other side for a hole-in-one."

He took aim once more, wiggled a bit, then tapped his ball and watched it slowly roll down the hill toward the windmill. The blade came down and knocked the ball back six inches.

Jessica buckled over with laughter.

"Yeah, yeah," he muttered as he walked over to his ball and hit it under the tunnel.

His phone rang as Jessica set her pink ball on the black dot for her turn. She paused and watched him on the other side of the windmill as he pulled it out of his pocket and answered. "This is Chad."

A breeze blew across the grounds, and she brushed her hair back out of her face. The serious look on his face made her wonder if their date was about to be cut short. He glanced her way. "Mm, hmm." He waved at her to go ahead and take her shot, but she became more concerned as the frown grew deeper on his forehead.

She went ahead and tapped her ball and followed it through to the side Chad stood on. She didn't even notice where her ball went when he asked, "When is the funeral?"

He glanced at her as she put her hand on his arm.

"Wednesday morning?" Chad asked into his phone. "Okay. And you're sure about the other?"

He listened for a while longer, then said, "I'll have to make some calls Monday to get everything squared away at the clinic, but I can come over on Tuesday. We'll figure it all out then."

Jessica kept her eyes fixed on his concerned face as he wrapped up his call. "Chad?"

He dropped his phone back into his pocket. "My grandfather died."

"Oh, Chad." She threw her arms around him. "I'm so sorry!"

He tentatively wrapped his arms around her as well. "It's okay, Jess. He's been sick for a while now. He had Parkinson's, and he was miserable that he couldn't make his hands work the way he wanted them to."

"That's not going to make you miss him any less." She leaned back and looked up at him.

"No." He shook his head. "It's not."

She stepped out of his embrace. "So, you're headed where?"

"Arkansas." He looked around the green they were standing on until he found his ball. "Where'd your ball end up?"

"Don't know." She scanned the area. "Where in Arkansas?"

"You stinker!" He reached into the hole and pulled out her ball. "You got a hole-in-one!"

"Chad, where in Arkansas?" Jessica wasn't about to let him distract her from the subject at hand.

"Oh." He fiddled with her ball, tossing it from one hand to the other. "Sassafras. It's up north of Little Rock."

Jessica stood there, stunned.

He looked up. "What?"

"Did you say Sassafras?" She couldn't believe her ears.

"Yeah."

"I know exactly where that is. That's where my Mom grew up. My Aunt Ruth still lives there."

"Wow. Small world." He flipped her the ball.

She caught the ball and closed her hand around it. "Maybe we should just skip the last five holes. I mean, it just seems so ... frivolous after that phone call."

"It wouldn't change anything. I want to finish the game. Besides, I promised you dinner and we haven't even made it to the concession stand yet."

"Are you sure?"

He stood right in front of her and tucked a strand of her hair behind her ear. "Am I sure I want to spend as much time as I can with you before I have to go to Arkansas for who knows how long? Yes, I'm sure."

"Why would you have to be up there so long?"

"Dad said I'm one of the executors of the will, so I'm going to have to meet with his attorney and figure out exactly what I need to do—see if I can do it from here or if I'm going to have to make this trip more than once."

They played through the last five holes, and Jessica's score was lower by ten strokes.

"That means I get ice cream too, right?" Jessica said with a teasing tone as he redid the math on the score sheet. She sat across the picnic table from him and pointed to a mistake. "Carry the one."

"I can't believe I got beat by a girl." He moaned over his basket of chili dog and fried pickles.

"You better believe it, buddy!" Jessica pointed her chicken strip at him.

"Sheesh." He shook his head in defeat and ran his fingers through his brown hair, spiking it up in places. "They didn't tell me you were so vindictive."

"Who didn't tell you?"

"All the guys at church."

"Uh." She leaned in closer, stunned. "They've been talking about me?"

"No." He laughed. "Just wanted to see what you'd say." He popped a pickle in his mouth and grinned.

She took a bite too, and then studied him. "Chad, it's a ten-hour drive to Sassafras. You shouldn't do that by yourself."

"It's not that bad. I'm one of these guys that just gets in the car and drives." He shrugged.

"But what if you start falling asleep at the wheel or something?"

"Jessica, who would go with me? It's ridiculous to try and fly up there. It's like waiting five or six hours in the airport for a two-hour flight." He wiped his mouth with the corner of his napkin.

"I haven't seen my aunt in a while. I could ride with you and stay with her. I mean, then if you needed a break from driving, I could drive or just give you someone to talk to." Jessica focused on her last two chicken strips instead of meeting his gaze. *Too forward, Jessica Garcia. What are you doing? You've only known this guy for a couple weeks.* But, in her head, she also retraced just how hard it had been when she made a similar trip by herself, and her heart refused to take back her offer.

He didn't say anything for so long, she finally looked up.

"Jessica, that's sweet, but you don't have to do that. I'll be okay."

"I know I don't." She lifted her chin. "But I remember how I felt when my grandpa died a year ago and how hard it was for me to have to travel all alone to Arkansas. I just don't want you to have to go through that, too."

"I don't even know for sure how long I'll be gone. I'm going to close my clinic through next weekend and see if I need to do it for longer once I get up there. I mean, what if I end up staying half a month?"

"Then, I can always get a flight back and have Courtney pick me up. I'll work something out."

He studied her for a few seconds with those sea-blue eyes until she squirmed in her seat, uncomfortable with his direct gaze. Her fingers mindlessly shredded one of her chicken strips. "Unless you don't want me to come with you."

He reached across the table and took her hands in his. "I have loved getting to know you this last week. And I look forward to getting to know you even better in the ones coming up. And if you don't talk me into this, I will miss you while I'm up there and wonder what I would have learned about you had you come with me. I just don't want you doing this if you don't really want to."

"I wouldn't have offered if that were the case." She couldn't take her eyes off of their entwined fingers. The first time she had seen him, his hands had mesmerized her, and she reveled in the way they felt around hers now. It was perfect, despite the situation.

"You really want to go?"

"I really want to go." She looked up and smiled. "I'll tell Courtney when we get back. Things are still fairly slow at the store right now and won't pick up until around Thanksgiving."

"What about Lester?"

She propped her chin on her hand. "Lester." Was Chad trying to get her to back out? Every time she countermanded his excuses, he came up with another one.

"You know, the cute cat I let you take home the other day?"

"Yes." She wrinkled her nose at him. "I know who Lester is. I just don't know if Courtney will be okay with me leaving him. He's spent the last couple of nights in my bathroom crying at me."

Chad laughed. "Maybe you should let him stay out tonight and see if it goes better?"

"You're not getting rid of me that easily. I'll figure something out." She gave a curt nod.

A grin spread slowly across his face, starting at the right side. "Then, I'll look forward to having your company."

Hours in the car together to talk and not have anything in the way of growing closer looked better every second.

***

"Are you nuts?" Courtney followed Jessica into her bedroom later that evening.

"You're the one who told me to date him." Jessica tossed her words over her shoulder. "Remember?"

"Yeah, date him. Not run off to another state with him!"

Jessica turned from gathering her laundry. "You make it sound like we're going to Vegas. It's Arkansas. And it's not like we're going to be staying in a hotel together. I'm staying with my aunt. We're going up for his grandfather's funeral. It's not like this is some romantic getaway."

"But you're driving ten hours with him. What do you even know about this guy?"

"Courtney, he's really sweet. I told him a little about Austin the other day, and he said we could go as slow as I needed to. He must be really great—he takes care of animals all day long. He cares about them enough to take them off the streets when they're left in the alley behind his clinic."

"And then passes them off to bookstore owners." Courtney crossed her arms.

"He's a Christian." Jessica hefted the basket onto her hip.

Courtney perched on the edge of the dresser. "Jess, so was Austin."

Jessica dropped her clothesbasket down on the floor. "What's your deal, Courtney? You wanted me to go out and date again. You wanted me to try this out and see if it would work again. And now you're telling me I'm being stupid?"

"Jessica—"

"I'm going. I'm sorry to leave the shop with you, but if he needs to stay up there for longer than the next weekend, I'll buy tickets and fly back. You'll pick me up from the airport, right?"

"Of course I will." Courtney sighed. "I just want you to be careful. You're like the sister I never had, and I don't want to see you hurt again."

Jessica plopped down on the bed beside her roommate. "You said so yourself, he's not Austin. I promise to be careful. And he shouldn't have to go up there by himself. It was awful when I had to go to my grandfather's funeral alone last year."

"Sometimes I think you're too nice." Courtney squeezed Jessica's shoulders just as Lester walked in and rubbed around their ankles.

"Will you be okay having Lester around, too?" Jessica picked the cat up, and he immediately started purring.

Courtney leaned over to look in the feline's eyes. "I guess he'll have to keep me company while you're gone. Maybe I can teach him to do inventory."

They laughed together, and Jessica knew that even though Courtney would still worry, she wouldn't worry as much.

~1979~

Ruth snapped their picture, but her face was angry. She glared at Sandy and Rob as they posed in their fancy attire, ready for prom. Sandy was like a princess in her bright pink dress with fabric roses all along the shoulder straps and a fluffy skirt that ended just above her ankles. Debonair in his tuxedo, Rob had his brown hair combed down and kept that way with enough hairspray that it was shiny. Her curls bounced as she swung her head to look at him again.

"Sandy, how am I supposed to take your pictures when you keep moving?" Ruth scowled.

"Sorry, Ruthie." Sandy rocked back and forth on her silver high heels. "I'm just so excited. We're going to be the best-looking couple there!"

"You're going to be a late couple there if you don't let me finish taking these pictures for Mom. Too bad Grandma had to have surgery. Then Mom could be here to do this, and I wouldn't have to put up with such nonsense," Ruth grumbled.

"Ah, Ruth. You've got enough pictures now. It'll be okay. Mom will be able to see what we looked like, and we'll have something to look back on to remember this night." Sandy looked up into Rob's blue eyes, preferring to get lost in their adoring gaze than to look at the camera anymore.

Ruth put the camera on the table and pulled Sandy by the arm into the kitchen, calling over her shoulder, "I'm just going to borrow her for a minute."

Sandy shrugged back at Rob before she was all the way into the other room.

"Sandy, I can't stop you from going, but I am going to warn you. People do stupid things on prom night. Be smart. Don't do anything you'll regret for the rest of your life. Just because you think he loves you, it doesn't mean—"

Sandy slapped her. "How dare you! We are Christians. Rob wouldn't do anything like that and you know it," she hissed between clenched teeth as she held back angry tears. "Just because you don't like him doesn't mean you can just insinuate whatever you want. He's a good guy. We're going to prom to have fun with our friends, and then he'll bring me home again."

"Just remember what I said." Ruth rubbed her cheek. "People do stupid things on prom night."

Sandy spun on her heel and marched back to the living room. "Let's go, Rob."

He looked over his shoulder as Sandy dragged him to the door. "Everything okay?"

"My sister is just being an idiot." Sandy made sure her reply was loud enough for Ruth to hear.

She stormed out of the house and stomped down the steps. Rob held the car door for Sandy, but he looked from her to the house with a concerned expression. Sandy wiped a tear off her cheek before it could smudge her makeup.

Chapter Six

~2011~

A few days later, Jessica jerked awake as the car stopped. She looked out the window to see Little Rock in front of her. Chad tapped his fingers on the wheel to the country song on the radio.

"Sorry I fell asleep." Jessica wiped her eyes and shifted in her seat.

"No worries." He glanced over at her before returning his gaze to the road. "You were only out for like an hour or so."

"But it's not fair to you. I came along so you wouldn't fall asleep and I did instead."

"But I didn't." He quirked an eyebrow.

She smiled. "We've only got another hour or so, right?"

"Depending on this traffic. We had to hit Little Rock at five in the evening."

"Need to stop and take a break before we do the last stretch?"

"I'm good until we get there unless you need a break." He skillfully cut around a slow-moving car.

"I could use a stretch break, but I can survive without it," she said as he changed lanes again.

"Want to pick up a sandwich or is your aunt expecting you for dinner?"

She glanced at the clock. "I don't think she knew exactly when to expect me. What about your family? Are they going to have food for you when we get there?"

"I'm going to drop you off at your aunt's and go straight to the visitation. They'll probably have some food there for the family."

"I had forgotten about visitation." She studied his face to see if she could read what he thought, but he was focused on the road and gave nothing away. "Do you want me to go with you?"

He gave a slight shake of his head. "It would be rather boring for you. Just a bunch of my crazy family standing around talking about Grandfather."

"So, what did we decide about a sandwich?"

"It's up to you." He gave a shrug.

"Okay. Find a fast food place, and we'll at least get a drink. Something to get us through the last hour."

He nodded and steered into the right lane so he could take the exit. Once they were settled back in the car with drinks and apple pies, the traffic had actually gotten worse. Chad carefully pulled back into the midst of rush-hour gridlock and inched their way north again.

"So, tell me about your grandfather," Jessica said around a mouthful of pie.

Chad glanced over at her and then back at the road. "What would you like to know?"

She took a sip to wash down the bite. "I don't know. Are you like him? What are your favorite memories? Did he laugh a lot? Did he like animals?"

He chuckled. "I don't think I'm like him, but he was a good man ... the first one in our family to be a Christian. Favorite memories are a little harder. My dad refused to live in the same town as his dad. He said he had memories there he didn't want to face."

Refused to live in the same town? That seemed odd to Jessica. She would have loved to live in the same town as her grandparents when she was growing up.

"Anyway, that meant we only got to see him once or twice a year, so it was really special when we did. He loved to make peanut brittle, and I would beg to help him. He'd stand me on a chair next to him at the counter so I could help him measure. He used to tell really fun stories of when he was growing up on a farm and had to help catch chickens, or they'd have watermelon seed spitting contests in the backyard. And he'd pull out his old army cots for us to sleep on when we visited and then tickle our feet if we didn't get up as soon as he thought we should."

Jessica laughed.

"If I ever did anything wrong, I remember him pulling me aside and having a little talk with me." Chad's voice wavered a little. "And I never wanted that to happen because disappointing him was the worst thing in the world."

She put her hand on his arm. "He sounds wonderful."

"He was."

It was quiet in the car for a while as they headed out of Little Rock toward Sassafras. The road slowly narrowed and started getting a bit curvier as they entered the foothills of the Ozarks. The leaves on the trees still had some fall colors on them, but some yards had more leaves than the trees did. Quite a few houses had flags and signs in their yards rooting for the Arkansas Razorbacks football team.

"I don't remember the rest of your questions." Chad broke the silence.

"Did he laugh a lot?" Jessica asked. "Did he like animals, too?"

Chad smiled. "Grandfather laughed more when Nana was alive. He used to say that she was the sunshine in his life. But he could still tell a good joke that had the whole family laughing when we all got together.

"As for animals, not really. I think living on a farm sort of ruined it for him."

They passed the *Sassafras, Arkansas* sign. According to it, the population was exactly 1,886. Even though Jessica hadn't been back since her grandfather's funeral the year before, things didn't look much different. The fire truck was parked outside the station so it could be washed, flowers lined the beds in front of city hall downtown on the small square, and Halloween decorations peeked eerily out the library windows.

"Are you sure you don't want me to come with you to visitation?"

"You said she lived on the other side of town?" Chad ignored Jessica's persistence.

"Turn right just across the railroad tracks." She waved her hand in the correct direction. "At least let me come to the funeral."

"You didn't even know him." Chad made a turn onto the narrow road. "Now where?"

"All the way down and take a left at the park." She pointed straight ahead. "I know I didn't know him, but I know you."

He glanced at her before he turned onto her aunt's road.

"Her house is the yellow one with the front porch up there," Jessica said before he could ask. "You said it's at ten, right?"

"I don't want you to feel pressured to come, Jess. Isn't it going to be weird for you to go to a stranger's funeral?"

They sat in the driveway. "I just told you, I'm not coming for your grandfather. I'm coming for you."

"But I'll be up sitting with my family, and you won't have anyone to sit with."

"That won't kill me." She raised her eyebrows. "Ten, right?"

"Ten-thirty." He finally relented.

She gave a little nod.

"Well." He motioned toward the steering wheel. "Did I prove I could drive okay, or are you going to worry if I end up having to drive home by myself, too?"

She laughed. "I guess we'll have to wait and see how worn out you are then before I make any decisions."

He shook his head. "You're nothing like I thought you'd be when I saw you at that smoothie place."

"Oh yeah?" Consider her curiosity piqued. What had he expected? "Is that a good thing?" Jessica cocked her head to the side.

"I'm still deciding." He wiggled his eyebrows. "But I am definitely enjoying finding out just exactly who you are."

Movement at the curtain caught her eye, and she pointed it out. "My aunt knows we're here. Want to come in and meet her?"

"Maybe later. I better get to the funeral home. Do you need some help with your bags?"

"I've only got the one." She shook her head. "I'm good, but thanks."

"See you later?"

"Definitely." She gave a nod for emphasis. "If you need anything, call me."

"Yes, ma'am." He gave a little salute.

She opened the door and grabbed her bag from the backseat. As she headed up the front steps, Aunt Ruth opened the door and smiled. She wrapped her in a huge hug as soon as Jessica reached the porch. Jessica waved at Chad as he pulled out and headed back down toward Main Street.

"He didn't even open the door for you?" Aunt Ruth made a "tsking" sound.

"Aunt Ruth, I told him to go. Visitation has already started, and he needed to get to his family."

Aunt Ruth nodded and shut the door behind them. "Who did you say his grandfather was again?"

"I actually don't know his name." Jessica set her bag down. "I figure since there's only one funeral home in town I won't have to work hard to find it tomorrow. Why?"

"I didn't get a good look at him through the window, but something about him seemed familiar," Ruth said, her eyes wary. "Brings back some bad memories."

Chapter Seven

The next morning, Jessica pulled on a navy-blue skirt and a rose-print cardigan in blues and whites. As she came into the kitchen, Aunt Ruth raised her eyebrows. "Got a hot date?"

"No." Jessica helped herself to a muffin from the basket on the counter. "Going to Chad's grandfather's funeral."

"How are you going to get there?" Aunt Ruth peeled an apple in long green strips.

"I was hoping you'd let me borrow your car."

"You don't even know this family." Ruth set the finished apple aside and started on another.

"But I know Chad." Jessica picked a walnut out of her muffin and popped it into her mouth. "I'm going for him."

"Look, Jessie. I didn't say this over the phone when you called to ask if you could stay with me, but if his family is from here, well, not everyone from Sassafras is worth being around. Are you sure this boy is a good one?"

"Yes. He's been nothing but a gentleman. I'm sure he's from one of the 'good families.'"

Jessica used air quotes to emphasize how silly she thought the conversation was.

"Be careful." Aunt Ruth put her coffee mug in the sink. "It's supposed to rain today."

***

Even though Jessica didn't know Elbert Manning, she felt like she did by the end of the funeral. She got chills as several of the family members testified to his great faith in God, of him being the reason they were all Christians. His wife had brought him to Christ, and they had been married for over fifty years before she passed away. He had two sons, two daughters, ten grandchildren, and three great-grandchildren. She studied Chad from several rows behind and began to think that if he were anything like his grandfather, she better make sure he didn't get away.

He caught her afterward and gave her a hug. As people filed by them, Jessica caught sight of a woman staring at her and Chad. When the lady realized Jessica was looking her way, she blinked and shook her head, skirting on down the aisle. With a frown, Jessica noticed several other people give them second-glances and double-takes as they passed by, but no one stopped to explain the strange looks. Maybe no one knew Chad was dating anyone?

"I'm headed out to the graveside service with the family." Chad didn't seem aware of the attention they were getting. "Are you going to insist on coming with me?"

"Are you going to let me?" she asked in return.

"Come on." He grinned at her. "We can leave your car here and pick it up after lunch."

"I get lunch, too?" She put her hand to her chest as if she were shocked to be worthy of such an honor.

They walked hand-in-hand to his Volvo where it was lined up behind the hearse. A cool breeze ruffled the bottom of her skirt. Dark clouds rolled across the sky, threatening to drop their burdens.

It started to drizzle as they made their way to the cemetery on the south side of town and wound through the drive toward the center of the grounds. A green tent had been set up by the grave and the beautiful cedar casket. Chad pulled Jessica to a seat beside him despite the fact that she wasn't family.

Thunder rumbled and Jessica whispered, "I don't suppose you have an umbrella."

"You're the one who wanted to come," he whispered back with a smirk.

As the final scriptures were read and the last memories shared, Jessica watched Chad. The mist from the damp air sparkled in his light brown hair. Tears welled in the corners of his blue eyes, but only a couple slipped free to trace down the contours of his cheeks.

As the coffin was lowered into the ground, Chad stood and sighed. The rain began to gently fall. Jessica squeezed his hand, and he gave hers a squeeze in return.

"I'm glad you bullied your way into coming." He cast her a quivery grin.

"Me, too." She smiled and looked down at the ground.

Most everyone dashed through the rain to their cars, but a man who looked a lot like Chad strolled toward them. "Chad, your mother and I ..."

The man stopped and stared at Jessica. She looked at Chad, but he was studying the man with a concerned expression.

"Dad?" Chad furrowed his brows.

"Sorry." The man shook his head and focused on Chad before glancing back at Jessica again. "She just looks so much like someone I used to know."

"My aunt lives in town. Maybe you're thinking of her." Jessica cocked her head.

"Maybe." His dad's voice was unsure. "Anyway, we're heading back to the house. Are you coming soon?"

"I think we're going to go get lunch somewhere. I may come back this afternoon sometime, but I guess I'm just not ready to face it yet." Chad gave a little shrug.

His dad nodded. "We'll see you later then."

Jessica noticed as he walked away, his gait was similar to Chad's. It made her smile.

"So, know of any smoothie places around here?" Chad gazed out into the rain as if one might be right over the hill.

"I know of one about half an hour away." She motioned with her chin toward the east.

"Really?"

"Really. There's one in Searcy." She nodded matter-of-factly. "I used to haunt it when I was in college."

"Well, let's go then." He offered his arm, and she put her hand through it to dash to his car.

He turned the heater on as they drove east through the drizzly rain. His wipers squeaked a regular rhythm as they swished back and forth. She verbally navigated to a place that hadn't changed in the three years she had been out of school. It was locally owned and a bit kitschy, but that just made it more fun.

They walked through the glass doors and into a Hawaiian party-store paradise. Fake bamboo covered the walls, and the bar looked like a tiki hut with a grass roof hanging above it. Crazy masks were scattered on the walls in various colors and expressions.

"Wow. This place has some major atmosphere going on." Chad fingered a fabric lei that decorated the bulletin board.

"I love it." She handed him a menu.

They ordered from the lady behind the counter—who actually remembered Jessica even though it had been three years—and then sat down at one of the small tables which had a pineapple-shaped candle in its center. Rain pattered on the windows, and cars drove by on the wet roads outside. Quite a contrast with the summertime warmth inside.

"So, how often did you come here to have her remember you after all these years?" Chad drummed his fingers on the table. He seemed unable to keep them still.

"Every Friday." She gave a small grin. "I will admit, though, that I didn't discover this place until my Sophomore year, so it was only for three years, not four."

"That's so much better." He shook his head. "So, that's your system, huh? Get a smoothie every Friday? Now I know when to be at the shop back home."

"Gave it away." Jessica snapped her fingers.

The owner brought their drinks and wraps.

"I can't believe you ordered wheat grass in yours." Jessica shuddered.

"I can't believe you never get any fruit in yours." He cringed in return.

"Chocolate is a vegetable. It's a bean." She blew her straw paper at him before taking a sip of her drink.

He laughed and shook his head.

As they ate and chatted, they lost all track of time. He was telling her a story about how his grandfather met his grandmother when Jessica's phone rang.

"Jessica, where are you?" Ruth asked on the other end.

"Searcy," Jessica said. "We drove over to have lunch at the smoothie shop here."

"For four hours?" Worry laced her aunt's voice.

"What time is it?" Jessica motioned toward Chad.

Chad glanced at his watch at the same time Aunt Ruth said, "Four-thirty."

"I'm sorry, Aunt Ruth. We lost track of time. We'll head back now, okay?"

Chad had already stood up and thrown their trash away.

"We can talk more when you get here," Aunt Ruth said before hanging up.

"Did you break curfew?" Chad shook his finger at her.

"Maybe." Jessica shrugged. "I'm not sure what's gotten into her. After you dropped me off last night, she said something about how you seemed familiar, and then she was sort of distant all night. This morning, she acted like she didn't want me to come to the funeral, which is one of the reasons I came up here in the first place."

They drove back to the funeral home in Sassafras. Jessica stayed in the car a minute as the rain continued to drum on the roof. She really didn't want Aunt Ruth to "talk to her" as if she were still a child.

"Not getting out?" Chad watched her.

"I wish you could come meet her." Jessica fiddled with the seatbelt strap.

"Afraid to face her alone?"

"I just think if she knew how wonderful you were, she wouldn't be so upset about this. It's like she doesn't trust you even though she's never met you."

"You think I'm wonderful?"

Her face heated and she avoided meeting his gaze.

"I'll come by tomorrow." He rested his hand on the steering wheel. "How's that sound?"

"Or you could meet her at church tonight." Jessica suddenly remembered Wednesday evening Bible study.

"It's a plan." He gave a solid nod. "Now, go face the wrath of your evil Aunt Ruth who told you to stay away from strangers."

"Be nice." She smacked his arm. "She's not that bad. Just overprotective."

"I'll see you tonight." He winked.

She got out of the car and ran to her aunt's vehicle. He waited until she had left before he moved his car. When she pulled into the driveway, she saw the curtain flutter. Feeling like a guilty teenager, she straightened her shoulders, grabbed her purse, and headed in to see what her aunt would say.

Aunt Ruth hugged her fiercely, enveloping them in the warm scent of chocolate chips and vanilla, then stepped back and frowned. "I expected you hours ago. I had no idea you were going to eat, too."

"I'm sorry, Aunt Ruth. I didn't realize you'd worry. I guess I'm so used to not having to let people know where I am and when I'll be back that I didn't think about the fact that I had taken your car and you were stuck here all day." Jessica put on a puppy-dog face. "Forgive me?"

Aunt Ruth shook her head, but Jessica could see that she was trying not to smile behind that frown.

"You and your mom. You just can't help yourselves, can you?" Ruth tucked a strand of Jessica's hair behind her ear.

"What are you talking about?"

"You make those big hazel eyes at me and expect me to just melt and give you anything you want." She threw her hands in the air. "Well, come on. I made cookies, and you can have some unless you're too full from that four-hour lunch."

Jessica smiled and followed her aunt into the kitchen. "Chad will be at church tonight. I want you to meet him and see how great he is."

"Your mom says you've only been seeing him a few weeks." Aunt Ruth sat across the table from her.

"You've been talking about me to Mom?"

"We *do* talk. We are sisters, you know." Aunt Ruth picked an apple pie off the table and moved it to the pie keeper on the counter. "And you're part of her life, so she talks about you. Family keeps up with family."

Jessica shook her head and sighed with exasperation. "I've known him for a month or so now. He started worshipping with the same congregation I attend, and we began talking more at the hayride a couple weeks ago. He's a veterinarian."

"Well, at least he has a steady job," she mumbled.

Jessica shook her head. "You're going to like him, Aunt Ruth. I promise."

***

She began to wonder if she had misspoken as they stood in the auditorium of the church building that night.

"Why does she look like she's seen a ghost?" Chad whispered into Jessica's ear when she came to get him to meet Aunt Ruth.

Aunt Ruth stared at Chad, her eyes as wide as saucers.

"Aunt Ruth?" Jessica touched her aunt's arm.

"For that matter," Chad said as he glanced around them, "quite a few people look like that."

Jessica noticed they were getting a lot of the same double-takes they had gotten at the funeral. "This happened earlier today too, but you didn't seem to notice it, so I thought maybe I was imagining things."

"If you're imagining things, I am, too."

"Aunt Ruth, are you okay?" Jessica squeezed her aunt's arm.

Aunt Ruth blinked a couple of times, still keeping her gaze on Chad. "He looks so ... familiar." She muttered something about the past haunting her. "What did you say your last name was?"

"Manning." Chad studied her with a concerned look. "I'm Chad Manning. My dad grew up here ... and my grandfather was a member of this church for what seems like forever. Do you know them?"

Aunt Ruth groaned and nodded, then murmured what sounded to Jessica like, "Not again."

Jessica exchanged a look of confusion with Chad. She'd never seen her aunt act this way. What was the problem? She touched her aunt's arm again.

"Really, Auntie, are you okay?"

Aunt Ruth glanced at Jessica and visibly pulled herself together. "I'll be sitting in my normal pew if you wish to join me." She walked toward the front of the building.

Jessica frowned, turning to Chad. "I feel like I need to apologize for whatever that was."

"Don't worry about it." Chad squeezed her shoulder. "Maybe she's just having a bad night."

"Maybe." Jessica studied her aunt.

"You going to sit with her?" Chad's fingers grazed hers as he turned to look from his family to hers.

She glanced back up at him. "I think maybe I'd better."

He nodded. "I'm going to go sit with my family while I can. My parents and sister are heading home tomorrow after we meet with the attorney. How about I call you tomorrow afternoon?"

"Okay," she said. "I think we're going to go hit some antique shops in the morning anyway. Maybe I can get her to talk to me ... figure out why she's acting so strange."

"Well, hit the stores, but don't hit the antiques. They're fragile." He cast her a teasing grin.

She smiled at him. "Talk to you tomorrow. And I'll be thinking of you as you all go through the meeting with the attorney in the morning."

"Don't worry." Chad gently chucked her under the chin. "If all else fails, I'll give your aunt my puppy-dog face. That always works, right?"

Jessica smiled. "It worked when I did it earlier. Think you can make your face as cute as mine?"

"Hmm." He cocked his head and studied her for a moment. "That's going to be a hard act to follow."

"Tomorrow." She pointed at him before walking down to where her aunt sat. Aunt Ruth glanced at her but didn't say anything.

Perhaps staying with her was a bad idea.

Chapter Eight

Aunt Ruth hadn't spoken more than a few words to Jessica after service. She still wasn't talking much the next morning as they headed out to troll through the several antique shops in the area. Jessica thought about calling her mom to ask if she knew what was wrong, but her mom's relationship with her sister hadn't always been the best, so she held off.

"Isn't this like the china in your cabinet in the dining room?" Jessica tried to break the silence as she held up a cup and saucer with delicate pink roses on their edges.

Ruth glanced up from looking through intricately embroidered tablecloths and napkins. "Mm hmm. It was your grandmother's."

"It's beautiful." Jessica traced the scalloped edges with her fingers.

Chimes jingled as other ladies came through the door. The wooden floors creaked under everyone's feet as they moved around old furniture and stacks of magazines and dusty knick-knacks. Jessica scooted by a large armoire full of salt and pepper shakers to examine some vintage hats.

Growing up, she used to love spending a week with her aunt, going to the antique shops, and eating lunch at the old-fashioned tea room. She and her sister would play dress-up with some of the things Aunt Ruth had saved from when she and Jessica's mom had been growing up, along with Jessica's grandmother's wedding dress and a few old hats and shoes. Jessica wondered what had happened to a picture of herself and her sister dressed up in old formals and hats with lipstick and pearls on, even though the dresses were much too large for their pre-teen bodies.

That was the Aunt Ruth Jessica remembered. This one in the store with her today scared her. She had a grim expression on her face and seemed to be somewhere that Jessica couldn't reach.

As they sat at a table in the tea room—an old-fashioned hat and pair of shoes as the centerpiece—and ordered chicken salad sandwiches and cheddar soup for lunch, Jessica hoped she could break through the barrier her aunt had built between them. Jessica fiddled with the spoon she had used to stir the sugar into her cup of black currant tea. She looked up to find her aunt staring at her with a forlorn expression.

"I—"

"Jess—"

They both started talking at the same time.

"You go first." Jessica pushed her spoon away to force herself to quit playing with it.

Aunt Ruth took a deep breath. "Jessica, I have something to tell you that you're not going to like."

Jessica frowned, but waited.

"I'm not even sure how to say this. You're going to hate me, but it's for your own good." She flipped her fork over and over and over again.

Jessica leaned in a bit closer and picked up her tea.

"You can't see him anymore while you stay with me."

Jessica's cup clinked onto her saucer. Several other ladies in the tea room glanced in their direction, but Jessica ignored them.

"I know you think it's ridiculous, but I've known his family a lot longer than you have, and they're just no good. So, I'm asking that while you're staying with me, you stay away from him." Ruth nodded her head as if it were a done deal.

"I'm twenty-five years old," Jessica finally said when she could form a coherent thought. "I live in a house I bought with my roommate over a store I help run. I'm an adult. You're treating me like I'm sixteen!" She tried to keep her voice firm instead of whiny, but she sounded a little hysterical at the end.

The waitress brought their food, and Aunt Ruth thanked her. "I'm just saying that while you're here I'd rather you not ruin your life and expect me to sit helplessly by and not do anything."

"Tell me why—why do you think his family is so bad? Why do you think he's going to ruin my life?" Jessica leaned forward. "Give me proof, and I'll believe you."

Aunt Ruth chewed for a few moments and took a long drink of hot tea. Then, she folded her hands on the edge of the table and stared at them.

"Why can't you believe me without me having to tell you? I'm your family. You got your middle name from me. You've spent your whole life visiting me and sharing holidays with me. Why would you trust him more than you would trust me?"

As the conversation continued, Jessica began to lose her appetite. She pushed her bowl of soup closer to the middle of the table and picked at her croissant sandwich.

"Aunt Ruth, what I want to know is why you don't trust my judgment. You're not giving me any reasons not to date Chad, but you're also not listening when I give you lots of good reasons why I should. I know I've already said this, but ... he's a *good* man." She spread her hands out on the table as though pleading with her aunt to trust in her opinion. "He's kind, funny, handsome, and smart. He's a veterinarian. Even better, he's a Christian."

"You've only known him for a few weeks." Aunt Ruth pointed her spoon at Jessica. "I've known his family almost my whole life. The Mannings are not who you need to be running around with. Besides, your last choice of guys wasn't the greatest, so what makes you think this one is better?"

How could she bring Austin into this? Jessica clenched her jaw.

"You know I love having you here. You know you're welcome in my house anytime. But I don't want you seeing that boy while you stay with me." She took another bite of her sandwich.

Jessica could not believe her ears. She pushed away from the table and stood. Aunt Ruth looked up, eyebrows raised.

"I guess I better go since I need to find a place to stay. Thanks for lunch, Aunt Ruth." Jessica turned on her heel and marched away. What was she going to do? A walk was what she needed, something to clear her head before she exploded all over her aunt in the middle of a nice, sophisticated tea room.

What a relief they had chosen to go to the tea room in Sassafras rather than the one a few towns to the west. The thought of walking that far was too much, but a couple of blocks was more than doable on this pleasant fall afternoon with the soft wind and sunshine mocking her foul mood. The rain from the day before must have revived the leaves enough to show a bit more color because they nearly blinded her with their radiance as she stormed down the road. Normally, she would have relished a day like this, but today she could find little joy in the beauty. Slowing her momentum, she hung a right at the road in front of the railroad tracks and followed them up to the park.

She still needed time to think. To cool off. And she hoped her aunt was also cooling off, although she doubted it.

Maybe she should call Mom? She pulled out her phone, but couldn't bring herself to dial the numbers. What would she say? No one wanted to sound like a brat, complaining that her aunt wouldn't let her do what she wanted. But at the same time, it wasn't fair that Aunt Ruth had put this restriction on her. Sitting on one of the swings, her feet dangled above the slight puddle that remained from yesterday's showers.

As if they had a mind of their own, her fingers punched the button on the cell phone until she got to her mom's number and then hit "call." It rang for a while and clicked to voice mail. She hung up and swayed back and forth. Her aunt's car hadn't driven by yet. Was she still sitting in the restaurant, waiting for her to come back?

Her phone vibrated and she pulled it out.

Chad.

She hesitated only a second before answering it. "Hello."

"Wow. It sounds like you just lost your best friend."

She couldn't work up a good laugh. "I guess in a way I sort of did."

"Where are you?"

"In the park near my aunt's house." Jessica dragged her toe through the muddy water.

"Mind if I join you?"

Aunt Ruth's car turned onto the street in front of the park and headed toward her house.

"Sure. It should be fairly safe now."

Chad paused. "What's that mean?"

"Aunt Ruth told me not to see you as long as I was staying under her roof."

There was silence for a moment. "Wow."

"Yeah." Jessica twisted herself around and spun in a slow circle.

"Maybe I shouldn't come then."

"I need to talk to someone." She sighed. "I can't get a hold of my mom. My aunt isn't being reasonable. I don't know what to do."

"I'm on my way."

She hung up and continued to sway back and forth, not really swinging, but letting the wind push her. Soon Chad's Volvo pulled up and parked at the curb by the park. He got out and walked across the lawn to where she sat.

"Need a push?" He smiled.

"I feel like I've been pushed off a cliff," she muttered.

He leaned down so his deep blue eyes could meet hers. "I don't know exactly what's going on or why your aunt thinks you shouldn't date me, but we can get through this. Unless you believe she's right and that we really shouldn't see each other."

"No." She shook her head adamantly. "She's wrong. I just can't figure out what's making her act like this. And I don't know what to do. If I keep seeing you, I can't stay with her."

"Come on. Let's go somewhere and talk. I'll take you back to her house later, but you need to get away from the situation for a while. Want a rematch in mini-golf?"

"I beat you." She stood and dusted off her pants. "Why would I want a rematch?"

"Just checking." He took her hand and walked her to his car. He opened the door for her. She mentally added one more thing to her list of things he did right.

"Want to see my grandfather's house? I evidently get to go through it and find things to keep before we just sell the rest to pay off some of the medical bills. Then, the remaining money gets to go to the family in equal parts."

"I completely forgot about your meeting this morning." Jessica sat up straighter. "So, does that mean you're going to be up here for a while?"

"Nah." He turned back on the main road and crossed the tracks. "Most of the family has already gone through and found the few things they want. My mom wants me to find all the pictures and save them. And my cousin didn't make it down, but he wants the nutcracker collection that Grandfather would always pull out at Christmastime. Somewhere in the attic there's probably a hundred different nutcrackers."

"That's cool," she said. "And what do you get?"

"I haven't decided yet." He stopped the car in front of a little brick house with an Arkansas Razorbacks flag waving in the flowerbed by the front stoop.

He caught her by the arm as she reached for the handle. "Wait." He walked around to her side and opened the door for her.

She still wasn't used to such gentlemanly treatment. He led her up and through the front door. A girl about their age sat on the sofa, looking through various stacks of papers strewn over the coffee table.

"Anne, this is Jessica. Jessica, my cousin, Anne."

Both girls waved at each other. Then, Jessica did a double-take. Anne had long brown hair, big brown eyes and perfect skin. Thank goodness Anne was related to Chad, otherwise, Jessica might be jealous. But wait. She knew Anne.

"You went to Harding University, right?"

Anne looked up again from the stacks. "Yeah."

"I think we were in the same dorm."

Anne studied her for a moment. "You lived on the third floor, right?"

"Right." Jessica grinned. "Small world."

"Totally."

"You hungry?" Chad asked Jessica.

"Not really." She shook her head. "I mean, I didn't eat a lot of lunch, but I don't have much of an appetite right now, either."

He nodded. "Well, I'm starving, so I'm going to go see what all is in the fridge. You're welcome to stay here or come with me."

She followed him into the kitchen and sat at the little vinyl-topped table by the window. He rummaged through various casserole dishes until he found one that evidently looked good to him. While a helping of the broccoli cheese casserole warmed in the microwave, he leaned against the counter and watched her, his long fingers tapping the edge of the counter and his eyes practically swallowing her up with their depths. "So, did she even say why you shouldn't see me?"

"No." Jessica propped her chin on her hands as she leaned against the table. "She just said that you were going to break my heart—that your family wasn't good. She pointed out that she's known your family longer than I've known you."

The microwave beeped. He removed his dish and joined her at the table. "So, we need to figure out what it is she thinks my family has done."

"It's weird, right?" Jessica threw her hands up in confusion. "I mean, everything I heard today at the funeral said your grandfather was a great man. Your parents seem really great. You're great."

He caught her hand as she waved it around to emphasize each "great."

"Jess, thanks for thinking I'm great, but this is serious. Your aunt has a real problem with my family, and we need to figure out what it is. I don't want to come between you and your family."

Even when Jessica had been dating Austin, Aunt Ruth had never said things like she said today. How was it possible that dating someone better than Austin would tear apart her relationship with her aunt? With the back of her hand, she wiped a tear from her cheek. "I hate this."

He stood and pulled her into his arms and just held her while she silently cried. Part of her wanted to tell him about what Ruth had said about Austin, but she couldn't. That wasn't the real issue they were facing. She eased away from him, and he handed her a napkin to wipe her face and nose.

"You think she'll throw my stuff out on the lawn?" She gave a half-hearted chuckle.

"Do we need to go get it?"

"I have nowhere else to stay." She shook her head. "I'm going to have to go back there in a little while."

"Anne's here, too, if you need a place to crash." Chad motioned to the house. "She could be the chaperone."

"I'm sure that's just what she wants to do." Jessica gave half a smile. "Is she staying the whole time you are?"

"I'm not sure." He sat down and took another bite of casserole.

"That sort of ruins that plan." Jessica stared out the kitchen window, not really seeing the yard.

"And you need to work things out with your aunt." He pointed at her with his fork. "So, I guess we're back to figuring out what your aunt has against my family."

Jessica plopped back down in the chair and propped her chin in her hands.

"Would your mom know?"

"Maybe." She gave a shrug. "I tried to call her earlier, but she didn't answer. I think they had something going on this week."

He scraped his plate clean, but she could tell he was thinking because he had a frown wrinkle between his eyes.

Anne wandered in with a scrapbook. She laid it out on the table and pointed to a picture of a couple. "You guys are never going to believe this."

Jessica's phone rang. The caller ID showed that it was her aunt. She motioned to Chad she'd be a minute and walked into the other room.

"Are you coming back?" Ruth asked without even waiting for a "hello."

"Yes," Jessica said.

"Are you with him right now?"

Jessica glanced back into the dining room where he sat. She really didn't want to tell her aunt the truth, but also didn't want to lie. Then, she remembered his cousin. Maybe a half-truth first and see how Aunt Ruth reacted.

"I'm with someone I ran into that I used to go to school with. Her name's Anne, and we lived in the same dorm." Jessica chewed on her bottom lip, still trying to figure out exactly what to do, and feeling like a rebellious teen.

Ruth didn't say anything for a moment. "So, you're not with him?"

Jessica sighed. "Aunt Ruth, please."

"I suppose you told him everything, and now he hates me as much as you do."

"Aunt Ruth, I don't hate you!" Jessica sat down on the couch. "And neither does he. We just don't get what you have against his family. We're trying to understand."

Aunt Ruth was quiet a long time.

"Am I still allowed to come back tonight?" Jessica asked finally.

It sounded like Aunt Ruth sniffled before saying, "Will you be back for dinner?"

Jessica felt a bit of the tightness release in her chest. "Yes. What time do you want me there?"

"Six."

"I'll be there by six," Jessica said.

She took a deep breath and tried to get control of herself again before returning to the dining room. Chad seemed transfixed by something in the scrapbook, and Anne was staring at Chad. Jessica walked over to see what was so interesting.

It was as if she were looking at a picture of herself and Chad, except they were dressed in clothes from the seventies, and the photo was faded. She met Chad's gaze and then they both looked back at the picture, and then again at each other. There were slight differences, like the girl's hairstyle, which was long and straight instead of cut in a stacked bob. But if she and Chad put on bell-bottoms, they could be the couple in the picture.

Chapter Nine

"This explains why everyone keeps looking at us like we're ghosts." Chad pointed at the pictures as they flipped through page after page of photos similar to the first. Anne had given up and gone back to other stacks of memories in the living room.

Jessica shook her head. "It's got to be our parents, Chad. I know I've seen a picture of my mom in that same dress."

"So, your mom and my dad—"

"Obviously dated," Jessica finished.

They found a picture of their parents on prom night, all dressed up in tuxedo and one of the old formal dresses that Jessica had dressed up in as a child. She traced the picture and remembered how much as a kid she had loved that dress with the poufy skirt and fabric flowers sewn on the shoulders.

"Is this awkward?" he asked.

"A little." She glanced up at him. "I mean, my mom and your dad ..."

"Yeah." He gave a little nod and looked back at the book.

There was a picture of them in graduation caps and gowns. Another in front of a car. And then a newspaper clipping caught their eye.

"Manning Anderson to Wed," the headline read. A picture of Chad's father and Jessica's mother was under that and then some details about the parents of the bride and groom. Jessica struggled to control her breathing. Dating someone in high school was one thing, but her mom had been engaged to a man that wasn't Jessica's father? How could this be?

"Are you okay?" Chad leaned over and met her eyes.

She ran her fingers through her hair. "It was serious enough that they were engaged."

"But we both know they didn't get married." Chad reached over and tucked a wayward strand of hair back behind her ear.

"But engaged—"

"Is not married," Chad said.

She got up and paced. "But it almost is."

"Do you think this is why your aunt has such a problem with my family? Whatever reason they broke off the engagement couldn't have been easy on anyone." Chad flipped over another page.

"Maybe."

Nothing was on the next few pages of the book. Then, all the pictures of Chad's dad showed him with another woman, one who had Chad's long fingers. Jessica knew it was Chad's mom.

"It still doesn't explain everything." Jessica continued to walk back and forth across the linoleum floor.

"No. But it makes more sense than anything we've come up with so far."

"Mm," Jessica mumbled. "Oh, what time is it?"

Chad glanced at his watch. "Five-thirty."

"I've got to get back to Aunt Ruth's house." Jessica grabbed her purse.

"I'll drive you."

They were both quiet as they headed back to her aunt's house. She wasn't sure what all of this meant. Her mom had never mentioned having another love before her father. How could someone love another person so much that she went so far as to become his fiancée and then just break off the engagement and marry someone else?

"Talk to you tomorrow?" Chad held the door for her to get out of the car.

"Okay." She nodded.

"Hey." He caught her hand as she started to walk away. "Things will work out. Remember, I still haven't tried the puppy-dog look."

She gave him half a smile and then continued up the walk and into the house.

Silence hovered over the dinner table that evening. Aunt Ruth would start talking about little things, like the weather, and then there would be long periods of quiet as they ate. When finished, Jessica set her dishes in the sink and headed upstairs.

She sank into a bathtub of hot water, bubbles piled up to the top. She had a new romance novel to read, but the plot didn't hold her attention. Every time she read another scene, she pictured Chad as the hero—and herself as the girl he was in love with. She set the book aside and leaned her head back against the terry-cloth pillow her aunt kept for just such an occasion.

Her life had seemed like a romance novel when Chad walked up to her at Smoothie Heaven back in Honey Springs, but now it was more like a mystery. While her mother's failed engagement to Chad's father might have triggered some angst from her aunt, she still wondered if she were missing something. Her aunt was more upset about her dating Chad than would be normal for a situation like this.

It was still weird to think about her mom being so deeply in love with someone who wasn't her father. She had always known her mother had dated other men before she married her father, but dating and being engaged were two different things. Engagement was practically married.

Jessica sat straight up in the tub. There was no way her mom had gotten married to Chad's dad, right? She shook her head, but the idea wouldn't dislodge itself. Her mom was adamantly against divorce, always pointing out that it displeased God. There was no way her mom could have married Chad's dad because she would not have divorced him to marry her dad.

And yet, if she had … that would explain why Aunt Ruth was so against Jessica's relationship with Chad. They might be … related. She practically jumped out of the bathtub. She had to talk to her aunt as soon as possible.

~1980~

When Sandy walked in with that rock on her hand, Ruth knew. Sandy didn't have to say one word or show off the sparkling diamond. Ruth could tell and her heart broke. She turned away from her glowing sister, went up to her room, and shut the door.

Sandy knocked later, but Ruth didn't reply. Sandy came in anyway and sat on the edge of the bed where Ruth was curled on her side. A tear trickled down Ruth's cheek.

"Ruth, please. Tell me why you're so against this," Sandy whispered.

"It wouldn't do any good." Ruth sniffed. "You won't listen to me."

"You won't give me any reasons to listen to you!" Sandy thumped her fist down on a throw pillow. "This whole time all you've ever said is that I shouldn't see him. You never give me a reason why. I waited and waited for something to happen to prove you right and me wrong, but nothing has. I've been seeing Rob for two years now and he's so great. I don't understand why you can't see that."

Ruth took a shaky breath. "He's a heartbreaker."

"But he's not breaking my heart, Ruthie. He's promising to take care of it and cherish it for the rest of our lives. He's a great man and we have so much in common. We both want two kids and we both want to finish college even after we get married. We're both Christians and want to make sure that each other gets to Heaven. And we both love our families." Sandy touched Ruth's shoulder. "The only thing I can find at fault with him is that you don't like him."

"I never said I didn't like him," Ruth mumbled.

"Then, tell me why you've acted like it for the last two years."

Ruth shook her head.

Sandy stood up and threw the pillow at her. "You're the older sister. Quit acting like a child. You keep telling me I shouldn't see him and that he's going to break my heart and that his family is no good. But you have given me no proof! Admit you're wrong so we can move past this and you can be happy for me."

Ruth sat up and glared at Sandy. "If you marry him, I will never be happy for you."

Sandy stared at Ruth, mouth gaping.

"Never." Ruth locked eyes with Sandy and didn't back down.

"I love Rob with all my heart. And until you give me a good reason not to, I will marry him." Sandy turned on her heel and stormed out of the room, slamming the door.

Ruth threw herself back down onto the bed. She didn't want her sister mad at her, but she couldn't tell her the whole truth. She couldn't even bring herself to think of it anymore. She wanted to eradicate it from her mind forever. Another tear trickled down her cheek, proof that she couldn't completely erase it.

Chapter Ten

Rob and Sandy sat on the back row in the auditorium after church, waiting for the preacher to finish visiting with the few people left in the building. They were scheduled for their first pre-marital counseling session. Sandy smiled at Rob. She had no worries. They were the perfect couple.

Rob looked over Sandy's shoulder and frowned. She followed his gaze and noticed that her sister was talking with the minister. The seriousness in Ruth's face matched the emphatic wave of her hands as she spoke.

"What's wrong?" Sandy asked.

"Not sure." Rob shook his head. "I just have a feeling your sister is telling the preacher that he should advise us not to get married."

"Do you think she'd really go so far?" Sandy couldn't keep the anger out of her voice.

"She's been more than adamant in her dislike of me over the last two years, Sandy. If she's really serious about not wanting us to be married, she'll do whatever it takes."

Sandy looked back over her shoulder at Ruth. Even though her sister was against their union, she hadn't thought her so vindictive or spiteful as to talk to the preacher about them behind their backs. Could Rob be right? She wanted him to be wrong. Maybe Ruth was just having a problem and needed Mr. Glen's advice.

Ruth glanced over their way and then back at Mr. Glen. Sandy turned to Rob. His jaw was set, his lips pressed together. Rob, who almost never let anger show, was quite obviously furious. How dare Ruth act this way! How dare she ruin her perfect happy ending! She half rose from the pew, ready to confront her back-stabbing sibling.

"Hey." Rob took her hands in his. "We'll find a way to work this out. We've just got to figure out what's bothering Ruth and then see if we can bridge the gap. There's got to be something that will help us."

Sandy nodded, but wasn't sure. Ruth had been avoiding telling her what was wrong for two years now. She and Ruth had been best friends before Rob came into her life. Now, it was more like they were strangers with bedrooms down the hall from each other.

"What if we don't find a way?" she asked Rob.

"We will." A muscle twitched in his jaw line as he glanced over his shoulder again. "We have to. I don't want to tear you and your sister completely apart. If we can't figure this out, then maybe we should back off for a while until we can. We all need to have a good relationship. We have to spend Christmas together for the rest of our lives."

"I don't want to back off. She just needs to get over whatever this is."

He squeezed her hands. "We'll figure something out."

~2011~

Jessica trod down the stairs in her bunny slippers. She found her aunt on the sofa watching a reality singing show. She placed herself between Aunt Ruth and the television until she looked up at her.

"I need answers," Jessica said.

Aunt Ruth licked her lips.

"I know my mom was engaged to Chad's dad." Jessica hugged herself.

Ruth nodded reluctantly.

Jessica took a deep breath. "Did they get married and then divorced?"

"No." Aunt Ruth seemed to visibly relax. "They never actually got married." She flipped off the television set and patted the seat next to her on the floral-print sofa.

Jessica sat down and curled her legs under her. She could at least drop the worry about possibly being related to Chad now. But she wanted to know more. She leaned back and studied her aunt. The clock ticked on the mantel, the only thing breaking the silence.

Still, no one said a word.

"Why didn't they get married?" Jessica finally asked.

Aunt Ruth sighed and looked up at the ceiling as if the answers were there. "Something got in the way and tore them apart."

"Did she love him the way she loves my dad?" Jessica's voice broke on the last word.

Ruth gave a smile. "Maybe not exactly the same way, but she did love him. She thought he was the greatest thing since sliced bread. He was handsome and funny and smart and he loved her, too."

It was so hard for Jessica to picture her mom in love with anyone else other than her dad. If she hadn't seen the pictures and someone had told her, she probably would have laughed in their faces. Her mom and dad were soul mates. Every time she saw them together, it was like they were made for each other.

"How do you love someone so much that you get engaged and then turn around and love someone else the same amount?" Jessica asked.

"I don't know, Sweetie." Aunt Ruth's voice was solemn. "That's one you'll have to ask your mom."

Jessica paused another moment. "Did you approve of their relationship, Aunt Ruth?"

Ruth pursed her lips.

Jessica put her head back and faced the ceiling. "Aunt Ruth, what do you have against their family? I thought maybe you just didn't want me to date Chad because of what had happened with my mom and his dad, but if it goes back farther than that, it must be something else. Right?"

"I think some answers you're just going to have to get from your mom." Ruth patted Jessica on the knee and stood. "I'm going to bed. I'll see you in the morning."

Jessica hugged her knees to her chest, shaking her head. She let out a puff of air, releasing her aggravation at the conversation ending before she could really figure things out. There were so many reasons she didn't read mystery novels. She would much rather know the answers up front instead of having to wait for the end. At least she had gotten one answer she desperately needed: there was no way she and Chad were related. But now she had even more questions than she started out with.

She sat in bed that night with a spiral notebook and scribbled the questions running through her head all over the page. Why did they break up? What got between them and tore them apart? Why was Aunt Ruth against the whole Manning family? What if whatever broke their parents apart broke her and Chad apart, too?

The last question terrified her.

Her phone rang, breaking into her reverie.

"Hello," she said.

"Hey. I'm guessing you have a place to sleep tonight," Chad's voice said on the other end.

She gave a little laugh and circled the last question on her page. "Yes."

"So, was it because of our parents that your aunt didn't want you dating me?"

"No." Jessica tapped the paper with her pen. "I'm still trying to figure that part out."

"Huh," he said.

"Yeah."

They each sat quietly for a moment.

"I did confirm something, though." Jessica ended the silence.

"What's that?"

Jessica drew broken hearts along the side of her paper. "They never actually got married, so we don't have to worry about being related."

Chad's laugh was loud in her ear. "I didn't know you were worried about that."

"It just ran through my mind earlier in a crazy moment of panic."

"We are in Arkansas." Even without seeing him, she could tell he was grinning. "Sisters and brothers can get married here."

"Ha, ha." She rolled her eyes. "No way."

"I think I can have this mostly wrapped up by Saturday, and I'll probably go back down then," he said, serious again. "Need a ride?"

"Yes, please. I'm ready to get back to my own place where I don't have to worry about whether or not I'm allowed to date you."

"Just worried about whether or not you might be dating a half-brother, huh?" He chuckled.

"Hey, I said it was crazy." She shifted on the bed to get into a more comfortable position.

"When's your birthday?"

"August 20, 1986," she said.

"We couldn't be related. Mine is June 21, 1986. There's no way your mom could have had both of us within two months of each other," Chad said. "Besides, my mom and dad were married in '84. So, my dad wasn't married to your mom when I was born."

"Okay, so the logic makes it sound even crazier than it already did." She felt a blush creep across her cheeks, despite the fact that he couldn't see. "Leave me alone."

"Sorry. Enough teasing. I promise," he said. "I'll let you know when I decide to leave Saturday, but it will probably be that morning. Do you want to get together tomorrow or just try to stay on good terms with your aunt?"

"Let's play it by ear." She sighed. "If I need an escape, I'll call you."

"Got it."

"Good night, Chad," she said.

"Good night, Sis." He hung up before she could complain.

She smiled and darkened the bubble she had drawn around the scariest question on her page. Then, she filled it in so she couldn't see it anymore, determined not to let it come true.

***

Chad called about halfway through the next afternoon. Jessica cleaned the flour off her hands from where she had been helping her aunt make loaves of bread.

"I take it you're doing okay today?" Chad's voice asked over the line.

She walked into the hallway and sat on one of the bottom steps. "'Okay' is a good word."

"I'm glad, Jess. I don't want to cause problems for you and your aunt."

"We were just making bread for church. You know, they give it out to visitors every Sunday morning. It's Aunt Ruth's week to be in charge of that so we've got about fifteen loaves of banana bread baking. It's a good thing she has a double oven in this house."

"I bet that smells wonderful." He groaned.

"It does. Maybe I'll steal a loaf? We can snack on it on the way home." She picked at some flour that had gotten stuck to her jeans. "She said they usually don't need that many."

"Mm, nice."

"So, what are you up to? Did you find all the nutcrackers for your cousin?"

"Yes." He chuckled. "And everything everyone else wanted. The tea set for my sister.

The silverware to my aunt. The letters to my dad. The gardening tools to my other aunt. There's just nothing like seeing someone's life being given away piece by piece."

She could hear the sadness in his voice. "Need a break? I think my aunt could spare me for a little while."

"Nah, I'm good. I guess I just didn't realize how hard it would be to go through all of this stuff. I mean, obviously most of the clothes and stuff are being donated. And a lot of this is just going to end up going to the service center. But still … everything in this house was my grandparents', and it's hard not to have memories attached to it." He sighed.

"Did you figure out what you wanted for yourself?"

"I get his Bible," he said. "It's amazing. It has the family births and marriages listed. The pages are bent a bit at the edges, and the leather binding is a little loose, but the notes he made as he studied it year after year … amazing. It may take the rest of my life to go through it thoroughly enough to have the faith he had."

She smiled at the thought of him leaning over the heirloom Bible as an old man, having to put his face up close just to make out the words. Then suddenly, he would sit up and say, "Aha!" She laughed out loud as the mental image completed itself and then had to explain her thought of him as a geezer having a light-bulb moment. He laughed with her after she had gotten it all out.

"And was there a little old you sitting next to me in that daydream?" he asked.

She thought for a moment. "I have no idea."

"Sorry," he said. "I know you wanted us to move slowly, but I just couldn't resist asking. I figured you had to have seen it somehow, so you must have been sitting by me."

She swallowed. "I do like the thought of me sitting next to you in that image. Although, if I were, maybe it wouldn't take you quite so long to figure it all out since you'd have me to help you."

"Very nice." He gave a little laugh.

Aunt Ruth poked her head around the doorway and then ducked into the kitchen again. Jessica took that as a cue that her aunt was ready to have her return. She stood.

"I better get back in there and help with those last few loaves. Any idea what time I should expect you tomorrow?"

"Hmm ..." He thought for a moment. "Want to say around nine?"

"I'll be ready."

"Have a great evening, Jess. I'll see you then," he said.

Jessica strolled back into the kitchen where Aunt Ruth was doing the dishes. She grabbed a towel and took a mixing bowl out of the drying rack.

"Aunt Ruth, can you remember where Mom is this weekend?" Jessica scrubbed the bowl dry with the towel.

"Seems like she was going to help with their church family retreat, wasn't she?"

"That's right." Jessica put the bowl into the cabinet. "I've been trying to call her but kept getting her voice mail. I just couldn't remember if this was one of the weekends she had something or not."

"You remind me a lot of your mom." Ruth slowly moved the dishrag around the loaf pan in the sink.

Jessica glanced up from drying utensils. "How's that?"

"Just some of the things you've said about that boy over the last few days. They remind me of the things she used to say about Rob. Almost exactly the same in some cases."

"Like what?" Jessica plunked a whisk into the utensil jar on the counter.

"He's a Christian, he's a good guy, he's not who I think he is." Ruth ticked the points off on her soapy fingers. "Practically verbatim."

"Well, it's all true." Jessica shrugged.

"She thought so, too." Ruth handed her another bowl.

Hanging on every word, Jessica waited for more. This was the first time her aunt had dared open up, and she didn't want to jinx it.

"Anyway, I just want to give you something to think about before you leave tomorrow." Ruth turned and faced Jessica. "So, I figured I should point out that if you're so much like your mom and he's so much like his dad ... well, I just don't want you to put too much hope into this relationship yet. You've only been together a little while. He's practically a rebound anyway, with you only being out of the relationship with Austin for a few months now."

Jessica set the bowl back on the counter before she dropped it. "Why do you keep bringing Austin into this? It has nothing to do with Austin. I dropped that baggage like I should have years ago, and I am moving on. Chad is completely different. Maybe if you told me what you have against the Mannings I could understand why you don't want me to date him. Instead, you're picking apart my love life and telling me I'm like my mom ... which I take as a compliment, by the way."

Ruth sucked in a deep breath. "I just want you to keep those things in mind. You and your mom seem to be a lot alike, as do your relationships with the Manning boys. Maybe that means that it's going to end up the same way. I don't know. But I do know that you're jumping into this awfully fast for having just broken up with Austin, who was also a bad judgment call on your part. That's all I'm saying."

"Then, I guess I'll just say good-bye tonight, and you won't have to worry about seeing me again for the rest of this visit. Sorry I brought up so many bad vibes with you." Jessica threw her towel on the counter and marched up the stairs. She slammed her bedroom door and threw herself across the bed. How could she ever like Aunt Ruth again, even if she had been her favorite aunt before this week? How could she go from looking forward to tea rooms and antiquing, baking together and chic flicks, to wanting to avoid her at all costs?

Chapter Eleven

A very sleepy Jessica climbed into Chad's car the next morning. Even though he was right on time, she had been sitting on the front porch waiting for him for over an hour. She just couldn't stand being in the house any longer. Aunt Ruth had shut herself away in her room the night before and had yet to emerge. Jessica had left a note on the kitchen table, thanking her aunt for her hospitality and letting her know she was headed home. She buckled her seatbelt as he backed out of the driveway, refusing to look at the house to see if her aunt was watching her leave.

"You look miserable." He glanced her way, concern written all over his face. "You feeling okay?"

"I didn't sleep much last night." She ran her hand through her hair. "Pretty much none at all. Thanks for not saying I look awful. 'Miserable' sounds better than that. Doesn't it?"

"What happened?"

She clenched and unclenched her hands. "When we hung up, she decided to give me some last-minute advice about my relationship with you."

"So, did she finally tell you why she hates me?"

"No." She shook her head. "That probably would have been easier to deal with."

"I'm so sorry I came between you and your aunt, Jess." He reached over and took her hand. "I never wanted to do that."

"It's not your fault." She leaned back against the headrest. "It's hers."

He was quiet for several miles before looking over with a grin. "So, no banana bread, I'm guessing."

"No." She smirked. "I'll make you some at home."

"Sounds good to me." He winked. "Why don't you try to get some sleep? You look beat, and it would probably make you feel better."

"I thought I was supposed to be keeping you awake." She stifled a yawn.

"And I thought you figured out on Tuesday that you didn't need to." He chuckled.

She stuck her tongue out at him, but leaned her seat back and closed her eyes. Her head ached from lack of sleep, and the painkiller she had taken earlier that morning had yet to kick in. Maybe a quick snooze wouldn't hurt.

***

Jess woke up as the car slowed down at a drive-thru. She squinted at the clock and realized she had been asleep for over three hours. "Oh!" She sat up.

"What's wrong?" Chad asked.

"I had no idea I was asleep for so long."

"It's okay. You're cute when you sleep." He pointed at the menu sign. "Want a taco or something?"

"Quesadilla." She rubbed the sleep from her eyes and straightened her hair. "And a soda."

"You got it." He told the speaker their order before pulling up to the window. He handed her the bag and pulled out of the drive-thru. "Did you need to stop or anything? I didn't want to wake you."

"Couldn't hurt to stretch a minute." She rubbed her right foot where it was tingling from being tucked under her so long.

He parked, and she walked into the restaurant. After splashing some cold water on her face, she glanced at herself in the mirror. She looked haggard, but maybe the bags under her eyes weren't quite as big as they had been earlier. As much as she looked like her mom, her eyes were the same color as Aunt Ruth's. Studying them in the mirror, she wondered if her aunt even realized she was gone. Did she care? Would she ever let her come back? Did Jessica even want to? She patted her face dry with a paper towel and walked back out to the car.

"Feeling better?" he asked around a bite of taco.

"Some." She smiled and wiped a drip of hot sauce off his cheek with one of the cheap paper napkins.

"I told you sleep would help."

"Yes, you're very smart." She dug in the bag to find her lunch. "Where are we?"

"Texarkana." He backed out of the parking spot and headed into traffic.

She had just taken a bite of quesadilla when he asked, "Did you know you talk in your sleep?"

Food threatened to go down her windpipe, and she started coughing. He handed her the cup and then patted her on the back as she cleared her throat. She took a long swig of soda before she could even think of answering him.

"Courtney used to write what I said in my sleep on the marker board in our dorm room." She coughed again. "Some of it was rather silly, but I could always tell when I was really worried about something because she'd have it written on the board the next morning."

"Wow." He laughed. "Nice roommate."

"So ..." she asked tentatively, her cough receding. "What did I say?"

"Oh, you know," he said in a teasing voice, "just that you loved me and couldn't believe it had taken you so long to find such a perfect guy."

"Yeah, right." She pushed his arm.

"You don't think so?"

"Nope." She gave a little shake of her head. "I guess it wasn't anything serious or you would have told me."

He glanced at her and then back at the road. "Nah. Sounded mostly like you were talking with your aunt."

Was he hiding something? She decided not to push. She wasn't sure she wanted to know, considering all that had gone on this week. Hard to believe that a week ago she and Chad had been on the mini-golf course oblivious to any of their crazy family history.

He found a smoothie shop for her in Dallas. They stretched for a few minutes and then got back in the car for the last three and a half hours home. What a relief it was to see her old bookstore that evening. His tires crunched on the gravel as he pulled up to the backdoor for her.

"I'm guessing you don't want to go grab a bite to eat for dinner?" he asked.

"Not tonight." She gave him a sad smile. "Bed sounds really good to me. Way better than food right now."

"So, I'll see you tomorrow?"

"Definitely." She nodded. "I wouldn't miss church."

"Get some rest tonight. It's going to be okay. Maybe you can talk to your mom tomorrow night and get some answers."

"Maybe."

"I'm praying for you, Jessica. And for your aunt."

She leaned into his hug for a moment before she headed inside. Courtney was waiting at the top of the staircase.

"I didn't realize you were coming back today."

"Sorry." Jessica sighed. "I meant to call, but a lot has happened over the last few days."

"You okay?" Courtney's lanky form filled the doorway, her arms crossed over her chest as she studied Jessica.

"Can I fill you in tomorrow?" Jessica asked. "I really just want to take a shower and go to bed."

"Sure. You gonna say hello to your cat at least?"

Jessica smiled and walked over to where Lester was curled up in the corner of the couch. She picked him up, and he let out a small purr.

His brown eyes opened halfway and then closed again as she snuggled him close to her chest. "Was he good for you?"

"He's been all over the apartment. He discovered your bookshelves the other day and made it all the way up to the third shelf before he got stuck. Then, Thursday he made it all the way downstairs, and I found him curled up behind the counter. I guess he couldn't figure out how to get those short legs back up here, so he just found a comfortable and safe spot and decided to sleep until I rescued him."

"My goodness, you've had a busy week," Jessica said to her kitten. He purred a little louder as she rubbed his head with her fingers. "Thanks for looking out for him, Courtney."

"No worries." Courtney gathered up some laundry she had been folding. "If you decide you need to talk tonight, you know where I live."

"I'll remember that." Jessica headed for her room. "Good night."

"Good night, Jess. I'm glad you're back."

Jessica tossed her bag on the bed and set Lester down. She took a quick shower and slipped into her pajamas. She scooted Lester over from his spot in the center of the bed and curled up under the covers, wet hair and all. She would deal with it in the morning.

Only moments from when her head hit the pillow, slumber consumed her. Dreams came, too, every one with Chad.

"You going to hit your ball or what?" They stood on the mini-golf course, and Chad watched her from the other side of the windmill.

Jessica looked down to see her pink ball on the green. She hit it through the obstacle and walked to the other side.

Chad picked her ball up out of the hole and held out his hand. "Come on."

He helped her up onto the wagon and pulled her into a spot between their friends on the hay. The truck pulled them forward slowly, and she jumped as a chainsaw sounded right next to her.

"It's okay." Chad wrapped his arm around her shoulders.

A sense of safety blanketed her as she relaxed into his arms. She turned to tell him thank you, but it wasn't his face next to her any longer. Instead, Austin cocked an eyebrow as she met his gaze, his blond hair impeccably neat, his eyes mocking.

"Were you expecting someone else?"

She pulled out of his arms and jumped off the wagon, rolling on the ground for a moment before she could get to her feet again. Right before he got to her, she ran through a door and tried to push it closed to keep him away, her heart banging in her ears, her hands shaking almost to the point of uselessness.

"Come on, Jessie. Let me in. There's nothing wrong about the way we feel about each other. Why won't you give in?" He forced the door open, knocking her to the ground.

Unable to scream, she scurried backward as he pursued her all the way into the corner of the room. There was nowhere to go. How had she gone from being safe and secure in Chad's arms to this? She jerked her head to the side as Austin ripped the shoulder of her dress and *leaned over her, pressing kisses everywhere he could reach.*

Aunt Ruth met her gaze from across the room. "I told you not to date him."

Jessica jerked awake, her eyes scanning her surroundings. Lester stirred and snuggled into the crook of her legs. Her breathing slowed back down as reality set back in and she could admit it was just a dream, only to start it all over again when she fell back to sleep.

She swatted at her alarm clock a few times the next morning before her hand connected enough to stop the buzz next to her ear. Lester stretched and forced his head under her arm to demand a scratch. She lazily moved her fingers between his ears and over his back for a minute before she threw off the covers and sat up. It wasn't very cool yet, despite the fact that it was late October. The extreme heat of summer was stretching into the fall.

As she washed her face, she studied it in the mirror. The bags under her eyes weren't quite as bad as they had been the day before. She opened the door for Lester and padded over to Courtney's room.

Courtney's blow dryer blasted through the morning quiet. "Got any concealer I can borrow?" Jessica shouted, rubbing a hand over her tired face.

Courtney clicked her dryer off. "What?"

"Concealer." Jessica pointed to her eyes.

"It's not going to be a perfect match. Your skin is darker than mine." Courtney stepped into her bathroom and came back with a tube of makeup.

"It's better than what I have now." Jessica headed back to her room. She mixed it with some powder and made the bags a bit less noticeable. After straightening her hair and throwing on a dress, she joined her roommate in the kitchen for a bowl of cereal and a mug of coffee.

"You look beat, girl. If it weren't my week to drive, I'd insist," Courtney said around a mouthful of Cheerios.

"I had some nightmares last night. Just a lot on my mind right now." Understatement of the year, but she wasn't in the mood to hash out details yet.

"Should be interesting when you finally get around to filling me in." Courtney took another bite.

"Yeah. Soon, I promise." Jessica rinsed her bowl, watching the leftover milk run down the drain—perfect analogy for how her life seemed to be going right now. "This afternoon we'll have a gabfest."

"After you take a nap."

"Perhaps." Jessica gave a smile.

The girls piled into the car and pulled out to head west to the church building. It was misting and the wipers streaked across Courtney's dusty windshield. There hadn't been enough rain the whole summer and most of the fall to keep her car anything but dirty.

Jessica's eyes followed the path of the wipers as she tried to control the butterflies in her stomach. She hadn't been this nervous about seeing Chad for weeks, but for some reason, the dreams of the night before left a queasiness she couldn't quite shake. He hadn't changed, but his transformation into the dream-Austin made her want to see that he really was the same great guy.

She needed a distraction. She held up a grocery bag Courtney had carried out with her Bible. "What's this?"

"It's the candy for Trunk-or-Treat tomorrow night. I figured since we live above a store we won't have many trick-or-treaters anyway, and we might as well join the fun at the church building." Courtney hit the turn signal to get on the interstate.

"I completely forgot about that."

"You have been a bit preoccupied with things this week." Courtney lifted a brow.

"But still ... I love Trunk-or-Treat. It's strange that I forgot." She set the candy back down in her lap.

Jessica kept her eyes peeled as she walked across the parking lot and through the church building with Courtney. No sign of Chad yet. Instead of walking the other way, today Courtney came to class with Jessica. As strange as it seemed to have her roommate beside her, Jessica was also grateful for her being close. The dreams continued to haunt her and good friends were nice to have near.

"Remind me again how you get to come sit in a class instead of teaching today," Mary asked as they sat down.

Courtney shrugged. "Evidently, one of the teenage girls needed to teach for her Tabitha class. She and her mom have taken over my second graders for today."

Chad walked in and leaned over the chair in front of Jessica. "May I sit by you, or is this side saved for the girls?"

"It's saved for the girls," Courtney answered before Jessica could.

Jessica swallowed disappointment. Chad in person looked just like she remembered, no signs of Austin-qualities around him. His eyes met hers for a moment, as if to make sure she agreed. She gave a half-smile, as if to apologize for her roommate.

"Then, I guess I'll just have something to look forward to during worship service," Chad said and gallantly walked over to sit with Garrett and Kyle.

"Wow, he really does say things like the guys in a romance novel," Courtney muttered to Jessica. "Are you sure you didn't create him out of your imagination?"

"Courtney, this side isn't saved for girls." Jessica stuck her bulletin into the back of her Bible.

"I wasn't sure if you wanted him to sit by you or not." Courtney nudged her. "The way you looked when you came in last night, I thought maybe something had happened between the two of you."

"It wasn't like that." Jessica shook her head.

"Do I need to go apologize to him?"

"Too late now," Jessica said as Randy started class.

An hour later Chad slid into the pew beside Jessica. A sense of rightness settled over her as his arm brushed hers. "Is this okay or is your roommate going to chase me off again?"

Jessica smirked. "We hadn't had time to talk really and she wasn't sure if I looked as bad as I look because I was mad at you or something else, so she decided to play it safe."

"Wow. I didn't realize you looked bad."

"Oh, please." Jessica rolled her eyes. "My makeup doesn't cover it up that much."

"You just look like you've been through a rather emotional couple of days. That's all." Chad scooted a little closer as several others joined their row.

"You're the one who lost a family member."

"You sort of did, too." He cocked his head toward her. "Unless your aunt has apologized and made up since I last saw you."

She just shook her head.

He put his arm on the pew back behind her as the song leader called out the first number of the hymn they were going to sing. She took a deep breath and told her mind throughout each song to pay attention to worshipping God instead of thinking about everything else in her life ... including the handsome man sitting next to her with his arm around her shoulders. She heard maybe half the sermon.

"Can I take you two to lunch?" Chad asked Jessica and Courtney after services.

Jessica shook her head and touched his arm. "I promised Courtney I'd fill her in on the last few days."

"I'll see you tonight then." He grabbed her hand and gave it a squeeze.

"Definitely." Jessica smiled.

"You didn't have to turn him down if you wanted to spend more time with him," Courtney said as they walked to the car.

"No, I need some girl time. It's okay."

***

Courtney's eyes were wide as saucers by the time Jessica got done with her story, telling her everything that had happened over the last few days. They sat on either end of the couch, cross-legged with Lester curled in Jessica's lap.

"And she just told you to get out?" Courtney asked.

"Sort of." Jessica dug her spoon back into the pint of brownie-batter ice cream they were splitting. "She actually changed her mind and let me come back, and I thought we were okay again until the next evening."

"When you were making banana bread." Courtney hugged one of her long legs to her chest.

"Right. And she started telling me I needed to rethink my relationship with Chad because it was probably a rebound from Austin ... and he was proof that I wasn't the best decision maker when it came to boys."

"Harsh much." Courtney unfolded again, leaning forward to grab another bite of ice cream. "Austin tricked everyone, Jess. Not just you."

"But what if Chad really is a rebound?"

"He's not." Courtney pointed her spoon at Jessica.

"But what if he is?"

Courtney locked Jessica in a no-nonsense stare. "Jessica, does it really matter if it works out in the end?"

Jessica chewed on her bottom lip for a second. "No."

"Then quit worrying about it."

"Yes, ma'am." Jessica wrinkled her nose.

"So, that's all she said? She didn't give you any reasons for not dating him?" Courtney inhaled another spoonful of ice cream.

Jessica shook her head. "She really didn't give any reasons." She sat straight up and held both hands in the air. "I forgot to tell you what Chad and I found at his grandfather's house."

"Some dark, hidden secret his family never told anyone, but your Aunt Ruth found out anyway?" Courtney leaned forward.

Jessica rolled her eyes. "You've read too many mystery novels." She pointed to her left hand. "My mom and his dad were engaged."

"Like ... to each other?"

"Yes, to each other, silly. Back before either one of them met who they actually married. They were in college and had evidently been dating several years." Jessica took another bite.

"Huh," Courtney said. "That's weird."

"Extreme weird, is more like it." Jessica waved her spoon. "It's next to impossible for me to believe that my mom was once in love with someone other than my dad."

"You had other boyfriends before Chad." Courtney nudged Jessica's leg with her toes.

"But not to the point that I was engaged to them."

"You would have been to that point with Austin if he'd been willing to go down that road." Courtney cocked an eyebrow.

"You're not helping."

"I thought I was." Courtney licked the back of her spoon. "So your aunt is mad at you for dating Chad because your mom was in love with his dad?"

"No." Jessica threw her hands up in the air. "That's part of the problem. I still don't know why she's so against this relationship."

"So we have a mystery to solve." Courtney raised a brow, the back of her spoon pressed against her lips.

Jessica pursed her lips. "I guess."

"I assume you've called your mom?"

"Can't get a hold of her."

"Maybe she's avoiding you." Courtney jokingly held a hand in front of her open mouth.

Jessica laughed. "Now I know you've been reading too many mysteries."

"Maybe." Courtney leaned back and pushed the carton with the last three bites of ice cream toward her roommate. "I guess I need to apologize to Chad for telling him not to sit with you earlier, huh?"

Jessica laughed. "If you want to. I don't really have an issue with him right now, I don't think."

"You don't think?"

Jessica leaned forward and put her head in her hands. "I think my aunt's mention of Austin made him start affecting my dreams or something. I kept having these crazy nightmares last night where Chad and I were on a date and then when I looked at him again, it was Austin instead. And he was going way too far physically. And Aunt Ruth was telling me, 'I told you so.'"

"But you know it's just a dream." Courtney touched Jessica's knee. "I mean, Chad isn't Austin. He's told you he'll go as slow as you want. He seems really great. You like him. What's all the drama about now that you're no longer living under your aunt's roof?"

"I don't know." Jessica groaned. She set the empty carton on the coffee table and resituated her cat. "It just feels all weird now. How can things seem to be right and wrong at the same time?"

Chapter Twelve

Several from the Young Professionals group stood around chatting after worship services that night. Jessica leaned against a pew next to Chad. He had let the elders know that evening that he wanted Northside to be his church home now and everyone had monopolized his attention for the first few minutes after the final prayer. Jessica was glad he was so accepted by everyone, but she was also slightly eager to spend some time with him after her talk with Courtney this afternoon. She smiled when he finally turned to her.

"So, this Trunk-or-Treat event tomorrow night, it's a costume thing, right?" Chad pointed to the announcement about it in the bulletin.

"It's optional, but quite a few people do dress up." Jessica gave a little shrug.

"So are you and Courtney dressing up?"

Jessica shook her head. "Courtney's not really a dress-up kind of girl."

"I'm not a what?" Courtney asked from her conversation a couple feet away.

"You don't like to wear costumes." Chad pointed to his shirt.

"Oh," Courtney said. "At least if you're talking about me, you're telling the truth."

"What about you?" Chad turned back to Jessica. "Are you a dress-up kind of girl?"

Jessica looked up at him. "I do occasionally wear a costume for fun, if I know other people will be, too." Who was she kidding? She loved dressing up, but for some reason, she was holding back tonight. "I think it's fun to dress up fancy, but that's not really the kind of event this is. It's outside in the parking lot, and it's supposed to be cool. Basically, you decorate the trunk of your car and then kids come by and get candy from you. There's hot dogs and chips and caramel corn. You know, the usual."

"We're going to dress up as transformers." Garrett leaned toward them.

Amber rolled her eyes. "How are you going to do that?"

"We found some boxes and spray-painted them silver and then drew the faces and stuff on them." Kyle did a few moves of the robot dance. "It's going to be great."

"You could join the boys and be a transformer." Jessica cocked her head to the side. "Doesn't every boy want to be a robot?"

"They're not robots, they're aliens." Garrett shook his head, his voice laced with incredulity.

Everyone laughed and then started gathering their things to head home.

"We could get some red yarn and be Raggedy Ann and Andy." Chad walked Jessica out to her car.

"I didn't realize you were a dress-up kind of guy." Jessica poked him in the arm.

"I guess this is really the first Halloween I've had a girlfriend, and I thought it would be fun if we dressed up as a famous couple. I mean, Romeo and Juliet are too depressing, and they were the only other option for a famous couple I could think of." Chad opened the door for Jessica.

"I'm amazed you could think of Raggedy Ann and Andy."

"Oh?"

"Not a couple you'd expect a guy to know much about."

Chad stuck his hands in his pockets and ducked his head. "My Grandma made us all one when we were kids. And I figured it would be easy to find some red yarn and paint our cheeks ... you know last-minute costume stuff."

Courtney got in on the driver's side. "You coming, Jess?"

"Yeah." Jessica turned back to Chad, her hand on the door. "I don't think I'm going to dress up this year, Chad. But it's sweet that you wanted to."

"It's okay." He nodded. "I guess I'll see you tomorrow night. Save me a hotdog if I get off work late."

"Sure," she said.

He squeezed her hand before she got in the car. She waved at him as they drove away.

"You okay?" Courtney elbowed Jessica as they stopped at a red light.

"I guess."

"What's up? Because the normal you would have loved to be Raggedy Ann with him as Andy."

"I wish I knew." Jessica fiddled with the ribbon on her Bible. "I told you that things were feeling weird. Maybe if I can get a hold of my mom tonight I can work through some of this mess."

Courtney nodded. "I hope so, too, because Chad seems like a really great guy, and it would be a shame if you let him go just because your aunt is weird."

"Courtney—"

"Admit it, Jessica. She acted weird."

"Acting and being are too different things," Jessica mumbled.

As soon as they got home, Jessica called her mom. She answered on the third ring.

"Mom, I've been trying to call you all weekend." Jessica sat cross-legged on the bed.

"I saw all the missed calls," her mom replied. "What's wrong? Is Ruth okay?"

"Mom." Jessica took a deep breath. "I need you to tell me about Rob Manning."

Silence.

Jessica held the phone away from her ear to make sure the call hadn't disconnected.

"Mom?"

"Jessica, where did you hear that name?" Her voice shook.

"I'm dating his son." Jessica leaned back against her pile of throw pillows.

"Wow," Mom said. "Small world. Remind me again of where you two met. And why I didn't know his last name?"

"Maybe I should start from the beginning." Jessica played with a loose thread on her comforter. "Chad and I met in a smoothie shop a couple weeks ago and then he started going to church where Courtney and I go. Then, one thing led to another and we went on a couple of dates, but his grandfather died—"

"Oh no. Elbert died?"

"Last week. I went up with Chad for the funeral because when he told me what town it was in, I knew I could stay with Aunt Ruth."

"Right. So that's how you ended up at Ruth's. I knew you were up there with a friend, but I didn't realize it was Rob's son."

"So, I went with him to see his grandfather's house, and we found an old photo album, and there was a picture that looked so much like us it was scary. So, we started putting the pieces together and figured out that you and his dad had dated. Then, we found your engagement announcement." Jessica stopped to see if her mom would automatically jump in and fill in the rest of the story.

"It sounds like you already know everything."

"But, Mom, we know you didn't get married, but I want to know why." Jessica sat up and crossed her legs again. Lester mewed beside the bed so she leaned down and picked him up to rub his head.

"Did you ask your aunt Ruth?"

Jessica rolled her eyes. "Aunt Ruth went ballistic when she found out I was dating a Manning. She threatened to kick me out, Mom. I seriously thought I was going to have to crash with Chad's cousin."

"Honey, I'm sorry. I had no idea she was still feeling that way."

"She didn't really kick me out, but it was pretty tense that last day I was there." Jessica wiggled her fingers to let Lester bat at them. "I finally asked her about you guys and if you had gotten married or not, and she told me no. But she told me I'd have to ask you if I wanted to know why."

Her mom was quiet for a long time.

"What happened?" Jessica leaned deeper into the receiver.

"We just decided it wasn't meant to be." Her mom sighed. "I decided to transfer to a different college where I met your dad and knew he was the one for me. We got married and had you, and now you're abusing me in my old age."

"Mom, come on. There had to be a reason you decided it wasn't meant to be. You don't decide to marry someone and then change your mind just like that." Jessica snapped her fingers next to the phone so her mom could hear it.

"Why does it matter, Jess?"

"I don't know, Mom. It just does."

Mom sighed again. "Something came between us."

"Another woman?"

After a pause, Mom said, "You could say that."

Jessica was quiet for a while. She had a lot to think about still. If a woman had come between them, her mom's heart must have been broken. If Chad really was just like his dad, could a woman come between him and Jessica? She tried to push that thought out of her head.

"Is that why Aunt Ruth doesn't like Chad and his dad? Because Rob left you for another woman?" Jessica finally asked.

"No, Jessica. That's not what I said. I said a woman came between us. I didn't say he left me for another woman. He still loved me very much and I loved him, too. We just realized that there was a big issue that was going to make it hard for us to have a good marriage, so we decided that instead of trying to live with that for the rest of our lives, we'd split up for a while. The thing is, we both found someone else we loved just as much, and we moved on with our lives. We didn't ever get back to each other to try and work it out."

Jessica still had no idea what to think. It seemed the more answers she got the more questions she had.

"Jess, are things okay between you and your aunt?" Mom asked.

"No." Jessica let out a puff of air. "We ended on a really bad note."

"That explains the tearful message she left on my phone. I haven't called her yet. I wanted to get your side of the story first."

"I thought we were doing okay. We were making banana bread and then suddenly she turned to me and warned me against dating Chad ... and then she pointed out that my last boyfriend wasn't a good choice." Jessica tried to keep the hurt out of her voice, but she knew it crept through anyway.

"Oh, Jess. I'm sorry. If Chad is anything like his father, he's so much better than Austin. Don't think about that anymore. You move on and make your own choices. You're a smart girl."

Jessica wiped a tear off her cheek. Her mom had always been a good listener. While all her high school friends had made fun of their parents and refused to have anything to do with them, she had run to hers and confided in them. She could tell her mom anything and knew she would never be judged, just loved.

"I better go call your aunt and see if I can talk her down. Shall I tell her you don't hate her guts?" Mom asked.

"Of course, I don't hate her!" Jessica lifted her hand. "I just don't understand why she hates the man I'm dating."

"I'm not sure I do either, Sweetie. All these years, and I'm still not sure."

Chapter Thirteen

Jessica turned on her phone to read the text message from Chad. "I have red yarn. Let me know if you change your mind."

She shook her head. Lester batted at a loose paper spider half-stuck to the front of the counter in the bookstore. She would have to take down the Halloween decorations tomorrow and put up some for Thanksgiving. Focusing was difficult. How did her mom's call go with Aunt Ruth the night before? What did her aunt Ruth know about the Mannings that she wouldn't tell? Why did Jessica keep having dreams of Austin?

She sighed and texted Chad back. "Sorry."

Courtney brought a box of new books in from the back room. "You look like someone who just lost her best friend, except I'm right here, so that can't be it." They were restocking the shelves with the holidays coming.

"Just have a lot on my mind." Jessica took the box from Courtney and opened it.

"Whenever you want to talk, you know how to find me." Courtney pulled out several mysteries from the top. "Did you make the sign for the front door to let people know we're closing early with directions to Trunk-or-Treat?"

"I'll go do that now." Jessica rescued the spider by picking up her cat as she made her way to the office.

"It's okay. See you tonight," Chad texted back.

"Aunt Ruth is wrong," Jessica said out loud. "It's not that he's not good enough for me, but that I'm not good enough for him. I'm a mess."

With the sign typed up and taped to the door, she grabbed a candy bar from the bowl next to the cash register and went to find Courtney.

"I'm going to run to Smoothie Heaven for lunch. Want anything?"

"It's not Friday." Courtney straightened from where she had been going through another box of books.

"I didn't go on Friday last week." Jessica gave a little shrug. "I'm overdue."

"You know what I like," Courtney said.

Jessica nodded, grabbed her keys and purse, and headed out the back door.

***

Jessica's eyes surveyed the menu even though she and Courtney basically ordered the same thing every time. The hairs on the back of her neck stood up and she glanced behind her. A man quickly looked at the woman next to him from where he had obviously been staring Jessica's direction. She checked over her shoulder but couldn't see anyone else they could be looking at. She placed her order for a wrap to split with Courtney, and two smoothies: one chocolate and one strawberry-banana.

As she turned to walk out, her hands full, the guy who had been ogling at her rushed to hold the door open.

"Thanks." She gave him a little grin and continued walking, but he tapped her arm.

"Aren't you dating Chad?" he asked.

Jessica looked around at him and resituated the cups in her arms. "Um, yes."

"You don't remember me, do you?" he asked. "I'm Brian. We met at church a few weeks ago."

"Right." Jessica suddenly placed him in her mind. "You came that first week Chad came to Northside." He and the girl had both been in the group with Chad the first time she met him at the smoothie shop. "Haven't seen you there recently."

"Yeah. Been sort of busy." He gave a shrug. "Anyway, if you see Chad, tell him we said, 'Hi.'"

"Sure." Jessica nodded and headed toward her car again. As she walked away, she couldn't help but overhear their conversation.

"You were right, Beth. He's dating her," Brian said.

"What does she have that I don't?" Jessica heard the girl ask.

"Chad," Brian said in a flippant voice.

A glance toward the shop as Jessica got in her car showed the girl didn't appreciate his remark. Jessica turned the key and drove away. She wondered about Chad's friends. She had never really met them. What was his life like outside his clinic and church? Had he been dating Beth before he dated her? Even though they had mentioned her past boyfriend, they had never talked about Chad's former relationships.

***

Jessica and Courtney had decorated the trunk of Courtney's car with lots of fake jack-o-lanterns and ghosts made out of tea towels that fluttered in the Texas breeze. They were parked between a truck completely decked out with hay bales and scarecrows and a Suburban that had eerie black lights and scary music and fake gravestones with silly names written on them. There were all sorts of cars around the parking lot of the church building, plus several tables overloaded with hot dogs, chips, drinks and cookies, not to mention a face-painting booth and several giant bounce houses.

Chad walked up in silver-painted boxes. He had one on his head with the face cut out, two smaller ones on his arms, and two on his feet.

Courtney raised a brow and smirked a little from her lawn chair. "I can't wait to see the others."

"They're over there." Chad motioned over his shoulder toward Kyle and Garrett, also adorned in silver boxes.

A kid dressed as a superhero went up to Garrett, tugged on his pants leg, and asked him what he was.

Courtney burst out laughing.

Chad pulled his boxes off and stacked them beside the bumper. "Nice pumpkins."

"Thanks." Courtney motioned like Vanna White. "I worked really hard on those."

Three kids came up dressed as superheroes and said, "Trick-or-treat."

Courtney dropped candy in each bag.

"Want a hot dog?" Chad asked Jessica.

"Sure." She stood and meandered over to the food tables with him. They greeted several other people as they walked. It was only a cool night, not cold—perfect weather for kids to wander around costumed as everything from baby pumpkins to superheroes, to princesses and pirates.

Jessica grabbed a Styrofoam plate and a hotdog bun. "I ran into some of your friends at the smoothie shop today."

"Oh?" Chad asked. "Who's that?"

"Brian and ... I think her name was Beth." She picked up the tongs and put a hotdog in her bun.

"Huh." Chad's eyebrows rose a bit. "I haven't heard from them in a while."

"Brian said to tell you 'Hi.'"

"I guess I need to call him sometime and catch up." Chad piled chips on his plate. "He never did tell me if he found another church home after he decided against Northside. I think he really just wanted to say he was looking for one to impress the girls. Although I don't think several of them cared that much. We weren't really close."

He didn't mention catching up with the girl. Her heart leaped at that thought, confirmation that she had been jealous earlier. "So, you had just sort of met them and were hanging out that night you first met me?"

"Yeah. Brian had been to church where I used to worship a few times and asked if I wanted to meet up with them that evening." Chad shrugged. "After that time he came with me to worship here at Northside, he sort of disappeared off my radar. I tried calling him a few times, but ... well, I've been sort of busy."

She glanced at him out of the corner of her eye. "Busy traveling to Arkansas and back?"

"And playing miniature golf. You know, important things." Chad stretched his long legs in front of him as they sat down on the edge of the parking lot to eat. "Did you get a chance to talk with your mom last night?"

"Yes." She took a big bite of her hot dog.

He waited for her to chew before asking, "Well?"

"She didn't really add anything to the story. She doesn't know what Aunt Ruth has against you, either."

"Huh." He chewed a bite of his dinner.

"Yeah."

They finished eating and then moseyed back toward Courtney with a plate for her. She had been handing out candy while Chad and Jessica had walked around some, making the rounds of the other cars, snitching pieces of their favorite candy, and greeting other friends. Out of the corner of her eye, she noticed Chad's hand reaching for hers and then pulling back again. Did she want him to keep going? Did she want him to back off again? She didn't reach toward him, either.

Courtney accepted the plate and handed the candy bowl to Jessica. Jessica sat in her lawn chair next to Chad's boxes and dropped a few candy bars into the bags held out to her by a fairy and a policeman. Chad leaned against the back of the car behind her.

Courtney glanced at the two of them as she ate her hotdog but didn't say anything. Concern etched Courtney's face, a slight wrinkle marring the otherwise perfect skin between her green eyes. Jessica avoided her gaze and looked away, handing out more candy.

As the sky darkened and the number of kids coming by slackened to a trickle of teenagers, Courtney packed up their chairs and shut the trunk. Jessica dumped the last few pieces of chocolate into a plastic pumpkin, and threw the bowl in the backseat of the car. She pulled her jacket close as the night air cooled. Courtney turned down a bag of leftover hotdogs to take with them.

"Mind if I drive Jessica home?" Chad asked Courtney.

She shrugged. "Fine with me, but I think you should ask her."

"Want to ride with me?" He turned to Jessica.

"It's out of your way, isn't it?"

"Does that matter?"

"Evidently not." She shrugged again.

"You can help me carry my boxes." He gave her a teasing grin before tossing one her way.

"I'll see you in a bit." Courtney got in her car.

Jessica picked up the last box and followed Chad across the parking lot to his Volvo. He took the box from her and threw it in the trunk and then opened her door for her. As she was getting in, his hand ran down her arm and she tingled all the way to her toes. She wiggled them in her shoes as he walked around to the driver's side.

"Are you okay with just driving for a while?" He pulled out into traffic and headed back east toward the interstate. "I feel like we haven't really talked, and it seems like there's something wrong."

"I guess." Jessica rubbed her arm where his fingers had been.

They drove several miles without saying anything. He merged into the left lane and passed a semi truck as they traveled south toward Austin. "Are you going to talk to me or do I need to prompt you?"

"What do you want me to talk about?"

"You look like you haven't slept in a week, Jess. Are you that upset about your aunt?"

"I don't know." She leaned a bit toward her door and glanced over at him. "I just haven't been sleeping well. I mean, I fall asleep, but then I have all sorts of crazy dreams that wake me up again and again. I'm upset with my aunt and the things she said. Maybe that's part of it."

"What exactly did she say to you that last night?" He glanced over at her for a moment then back to the road.

Jessica took a deep breath. She stared at her hands as she talked. "She warned me again about dating you."

"And?"

"And she pointed out that I was a lot like my mom, who didn't end up staying with your dad, so I probably wouldn't get it to work out with you, either."

"Really?" he asked. "She said it wouldn't work out just because it didn't work for our parents?"

Jessica nodded.

"You realize that their relationship really has nothing to do with ours, right?"

"But it sort of does, Chad. I mean, yeah, we look like them, and that doesn't really matter except that it made people look at us weirdly in Sassafras. But I am a lot like my mom. My aunt was right when she said that. And I'm assuming you're a lot like your dad, too, right?"

"I do have some of his traits, some of his bad habits, probably. But that doesn't mean I'm exactly like him. And even if I were, just because it didn't work out for them, doesn't mean it can't work out for us."

Jessica stared out the window as they got closer to the city. She could see the lights of the university and the state capital's dome shining pink in the moonlight. He exited and made a wide loop through downtown, avoiding the revelers on Sixth Street, although every now and then she caught sight of a costumed person staggering away from that area. A few bats still fluttered around over the river in the moonlight before they re-entered the interstate.

"What are you dreaming that has to do with your aunt telling you to stay away from me?" He started north again, back toward Honey Springs.

Jessica sighed but didn't answer.

"Jess? Don't you think I deserve to know if you're having nightmares about me?" Part of his teasing came out in that question and then he switched back to serious. "I want to have a relationship with you, but it's hard to have a relationship when you won't talk to me."

"What, so now I have to tell you all my dreams to be in a relationship with you?" Jessica turned to face him.

"Whoa." He held a hand up from the steering wheel. "That's not what I said. I'm just trying to figure out what's going on. It seems like you're building a wall between us, and I'm not good at climbing walls."

"Sorry." Jessica lifted her hands and then put them in her lap again. "I guess I'm just worn out. I have all these questions running around in my mind and no answers anywhere to be found. And the nightmares aren't really about you. It's ... it's someone else who keeps waking me up."

"Someone else?"

"Austin," Jessica whispered. "Aunt Ruth said that I shouldn't trust my choices in men seeing how my past choices ended up. She was talking about Austin."

"Your ex-boyfriend." He pursed his lips as if the word were sour in his mouth. "That explains why you kept saying his name in your sleep on the ride home the other day."

She looked at him sharply. So that was what he had kept from her. Could she die of embarrassment?

"So, she thinks I'm going to be like him." His voice was almost a growl.

"Yes." A tear trickled down her cheek.

In the glow of the streetlights, his knuckles showed white from his grip on the steering wheel. He hit the turn signal harder than he needed to and got off on the exit for Honey Springs. He steered down the sleepy main street. Was he mad at her or her aunt or her ex-boyfriend ... or all three? She was afraid to ask.

He took a deep breath. "Jess, have you talked to God about all this?"

He went from being visibly angry a moment ago to asking her about her relationship with God now? Where did that come from? She stilled her thoughts. She wasn't really angry at him for bringing up God—she was angry that she couldn't answer "yes" to his question. She wasn't used to a boyfriend who cared about where she stood with God, and while it was nice, it was also uncomfortable.

He glanced over at her. "I know you're confused and worried about whatever is going on with your aunt. And you evidently have doubts about our relationship. But you can't let doubt rule your life. If you hold back and don't try anything new, how will you ever know if it might have been good or not? We're both Christians, and in my opinion, God has to be the main part of our relationship. Don't you trust God to take care of you ... and us?"

She took a shaky breath. Trust was a hard word. She thought she trusted God. But she had also trusted Austin, and that hadn't worked out well. She thought she had started to trust Chad, but now she had all these doubts. She had no idea what to think about any of this right now. Her head was spinning.

His tires crunched over the gravel as he pulled behind the store. She put her hand on the door handle and was about to open it when he reached over and stopped her. They sat there for a moment in the quiet, not looking at each other.

"I'm sorry, Jessica, but I think your aunt has major problems," Chad finally said.

"What?" She met his gaze.

"She is ... I don't know what." He hit his palms on the steering wheel. "I don't understand why she's against us, and I don't understand how someone who used to be so close to you could say something so cruel to you."

Jessica opened and closed her mouth. First he questioned her faith in God and now he was questioning whether or not her aunt actually loved her? Really?

"She's done this to you." He waved his hand in her direction. "With just a few words. You're not sleeping, you don't laugh at my jokes, you're having nightmares about your ex-boyfriend."

"And now the man I was dating is talking bad about my family," Jessica said before he could continue. Out of the muddled mix of emotional turmoil churning in her head, this was the thought that leapt to the front. He was attacking her favorite aunt. Deep inside, she knew it was ridiculous to be this riled about it, but everything was boiling over and the lid was about to explode. Something had to escape, and this seemed to be the easiest to deal with at the moment.

"Jessica—"

"No. It's not cool, Chad. I wouldn't go pointing out your family member's flaws."

"What flaws?"

"I don't know. I'm just making a point."

"All I'm saying is you can't let your aunt rule your life like this. No one even knows what she has against me. And yet, it's like you believe her anyway!"

"But you're acting like she's crazy or something." Jessica drew a circle in the air around her temple. "She's not crazy. She just worries about me. It's what family does."

"Yes, they worry about each other. But they don't go after people they don't even know, especially when they have no reason for it. It's like now that she's brought up her prejudice against me from some unknown past ...

something ... you won't even give me a chance to prove her wrong!"

"Well, you're not exactly doing a great job of proving her wrong right now!" Jessica yelled back.

"Are you kidding me?"

"No." Her voice lowered to just above a whisper.

He looked at her and she looked at him. She found the door handle again, and pulled it. The lights came on in the car, and she got a full view of his shattered expression. His eyes that she could normally stare at for hours swam with so much hurt she couldn't bear to look at them. She wanted to change them back to the calm oceans they normally were, but at the same time, she couldn't excuse how he had talked about Aunt Ruth. He may be hurting right now, but she was hurting, too. This wasn't easy for her. And he had just made it harder. Looking away from his torn expression, she forced herself to get out and rushed up to the store where Courtney had left the light on for her. She didn't look back as she shut the door behind her, but she leaned against the wall and listened to his car crunch down the driveway. Tears dripped off her chin.

Courtney opened her mouth to say something as Jessica walked through the apartment, but Jessica just kept going and shut the bedroom door before her friend could get a word in. Lester meowed outside the room, but she ignored him. Had she messed up one of the best things that had ever happened to her? Could she undo it? What had gone so wrong in such a short time? Just last week she had been joking with Chad on the golf course and now she wasn't sure he would ever talk to her again. Such a short drive this evening had led to such an emotional roller coaster, from having him worrying about her faith to calling her aunt basically insane. How was she supposed to just let the last part slide? She went to the bathroom and washed her face, put on her pajamas, and climbed into bed. And still tears ran down her cheeks. Now that she knew what a relationship with Chad was like, could she live without it? Or would they just be living up to Aunt Ruth's expectations?

Chapter Fourteen

~1980~

Sandy leaned into Rob's embrace as she cried after another argument with her sister. This was the third one in two weeks. They were three months from the date scheduled for their wedding, but the closer they got to it, the worse things got between Ruth and her. He rubbed her back as they stood in the parking lot of the bakery they were supposed to be visiting to talk about their cake.

"I'm sorry." She wiped her nose with an already damp tissue. "I just can't figure out why she's doing this."

"I know, Honey." He lifted her chin and kissed the tip of her nose despite the tears wetting it. "I wish I knew what to tell you."

"She's just being so mean. I had a feeling she'd have some issues with me getting married first since she was older, but this is ridiculous."

"I just don't think it has anything to do with you being younger. Something tells me it's another matter entirely."

"What, though? What could it be?" She swiped at her face with the backs of her hands.

"I wish I knew."

Sandy pulled several tissues out of a box in the front of her car and mopped her face and blew her nose. She brushed on powder to hide some of the splotchiness and rubbed on fresh lipstick. When she figured she was presentable enough, she got out of the car again and nodded to Rob that she was ready to go in.

They walked through the glass door, making the bells tinkle. A lady in a pink apron met with them in another room and talked with them about flavors of cake and flavors of icing and cake toppers and how many layers would be required. Sandy tried to focus, but her mind was still thinking about the argument she had had with Ruth that morning. Ruth had insulted her bridesmaid dress. That's how it started anyway.

When Ruth's opinionated comments changed from the cut of the dress—poofy skirts and shoulder straps—to the choice of the groom, things escalated. Then came all the usual arguments. She was tired of hearing how her sister thought that Rob was not worth her time of day, that his family was bad, that he would break her heart. So far, the only person breaking Sandy's heart was Ruth.

~2011~

A week later, Jessica still hadn't talked to Chad. He had called on the first day of

November and left a message of apology, saying she was right: he shouldn't have said those things about her aunt. The message was still on her voice mail, but she hadn't called him back. Neither one of them had handled the argument well the other night, but especially her. She kept thinking about what she could say to Chad, to try and explain what was going through her head, her heart. But she couldn't even explain it to herself.

Why was she so upset that her aunt was set against her boyfriend? She had defended him to Aunt Ruth with her every breath and now couldn't even talk to him. Was it because of her recurring dreams? Was it because her aunt's words kept running through her head over and over? She just didn't know. Sadly, the one person she couldn't bring herself to talk to about all of this was the one who she wanted to talk to the most.

She had avoided people as much as possible that first day after their fight. Instead of working at the cash register as she usually liked to do, she left that job to Courtney and organized the back room, moving boxes of books around to where they could find things more easily. She put up the Halloween decorations and set out some cornucopias, turkeys and pumpkins for Thanksgiving.

At church that Wednesday night, she saw Chad glance her way, but she masked any signs of wanting his attention. If she let him near her, he would probably want an explanation for her silence, or at least an acceptance of his apology. And even though she could almost admit he was right about how Aunt Ruth had acted, she just couldn't say it out loud yet.

He sat at the other end of the Young Professionals' pew, his grandfather's Bible open in his lap. She ignored the looks she got from the others on their row. That Sunday had been the same way. Jessica tried not to overhear the conversations around her.

"What's up with Jessica and Chad?" Amber whispered to Courtney. "Think I could try my hand at catching Chad's attention? Is Jessica still in love with him?"

Jessica didn't stick around to hear Courtney's answer. She had a feeling her roommate would suggest Amber back off, but she shouldn't have to say it anyway. Right? Weren't couples allowed to fight for a week without having people assume they had broken up?

She forced her breathing to remain in a regular rhythm. Had she and Chad even been together long enough to be considered a couple? They had only had two dates and a trip to Arkansas. Did she have enough claim on him to keep Amber from moving in? She glanced back over her shoulder at Amber. If Jessica took too long to figure this all out, would he consider moving on?

Chad's clinic called her a week after their fight. The receptionist informed her that they figured Lester was about four months old now and needed his shots and to be neutered soon.

"Would you like to make an appointment?"

Jessica wavered on her answer. She would be a bad pet parent if she didn't take care of her cat, but if she brought Lester in, she might run into Chad as well. She wanted to see him, but still wasn't sure what to say. Would he even want to see her? Even though he had glanced her way a few times at church, he hadn't actually come over to talk. Maybe she could get Courtney to take Lester. She shook her head. This was ridiculous! She was a grown woman. She could handle this. With a sigh, she agreed to bring Lester in Tuesday morning.

She loaded Lester into the cardboard box and drove him down to Chad's clinic. She filled out the forms with her information for the receptionist and let her take the sad kitty. He mewed pitifully from inside his box and scratched at the corners as he tried to find a way out. Jessica left quickly, before she ran the risk of running into the veterinarian himself.

The bells jingled as she came back that afternoon to get her pet. The reception area was empty. It was a nerve wracking minute before the receptionist came out to help her.

"Lester, right?" the receptionist asked.

"Right." Jessica repositioned her purse strap.

"It'll just be a moment. Dr. Manning is finishing up with a patient and then he'll meet with you to show you how to take care of Lester as he heals."

Jessica sat down on one of the plastic chairs against the wall. An occasional bark sounded in the back. Chad's laughter came from one of the exam rooms and her heart clenched a bit. He had a great sense of humor and she had just pushed it away. She shifted her weight, watched the fish in the aquarium, blankly studied the posters on why animals should be neutered.

Before she was ready, and after it seemed like she had waited forever, he came out. He looked so good, his hair combed in that way he had of making it look messy and put together at the same time, his white jacket showing off his broad shoulders. Just like the first time she had seen him, her heart betrayed her by speeding up. She searched his eyes, wanted to see if he maybe still felt the attraction she did, but he quickly turned and headed back into the hallway. She stood on shaky legs and followed him back to one of the exam rooms. Lester lay on a towel on the table. He looked up at her with his brown eyes and mewed a little. She rubbed his head.

"Lester will be sore for a few days and probably shouldn't jump much if you can keep him from it." Chad reached over to rub the cat's head and Jessica jerked her hand away, almost regretting not letting their fingers touch.

"I'll try to keep him locked away again so he won't go up and down the stairs," she said.

"I'm going to give you a couple days' worth of antibiotics. Do you know how to give them to him?"

Jessica shook her head.

"Just grab him by the ears and the neck here and pull his head back until he opens his mouth. It won't hurt him, but if you can get his mouth open and get the pill in far enough, he won't spit it back out. If that doesn't work, you can mush it up and mix it with some tuna or wet food."

"I'm guessing I can't just get you to give him his pill every day?" Jessica fell back into her teasing mode as if they had never had a fight. She realized what she had done and looked up to meet his gaze. "Sorry."

"Sorry for what?"

"I don't know."

"Then you're not really sorry," he said quietly. "Did you get my message the other day?"

She took a deep breath. "Yes."

"So, you know why I'm sorry," he whispered.

After a moment, she nodded. "So, keep him from jumping and stuff a pill in his throat. Anything else?"

Chad sighed and stared at her for a moment. "Just watch him. If you see the wound oozing or looking worse, bring him back in and we'll look at it. But he should be fine."

"How much do I owe you?"

He didn't answer for so long that she looked up again.

"I would say the original payment offer still stands, but something tells me you're not going to want to hear that."

Part of Jessica did want to hear it. Why couldn't things go back to the way they had been before Arkansas? When they had just started to get to know each other and could tease and flirt and just be themselves. Instead, she forced her heart back into submission and shook her head in answer to his statement. Until she could talk to him, really talk to him, they couldn't go back to where they had been. There was just too much hanging in the air ... too many unanswered questions.

"Honestly, it's my fault you have this cat in the first place. You took him off my hands. I would have done all this stuff for him anyway. Don't worry about it." Chad turned and left the room before she could protest. She stared at the door for a long moment, her heart breaking all over again. She wanted to be able to give Chad what he wanted ... to accept his apology and give him one of her own, but something held her back. She was so afraid of living up to her aunt's expectations, of getting deeper into this relationship only to see it fail. But, at the same time, isn't *failing* what they were doing now as she continued to hold him at a distance?

Lester's mewl brought her back to the present. She stuck the bottle of pills in her purse and gently laid her cat back in his box. She stopped by the receptionist's desk on the way out, but the girl confirmed that Dr. Manning had declared this visit free-of-charge.

With a sigh, Jessica left the clinic. A huge piece of her heart stayed inside—despite the brevity of their acquaintance, she missed Chad like crazy. If only she knew the right answers! Would knowing why their parents had broken up help her get over her fear of dating Chad?

***

Thursday evening the following week, she sat at Smoothie Heaven. Since Chad had figured out her normal night to come, she had switched it. Not long after she claimed a table out on the patio to enjoy the cool weather, he straddled one of the chairs across from her.

"I've been coming every night for the last week trying to find you." Instead of the self-confident man who had first introduced himself to her here, his unkempt hair and furrowed brow made him appear unsure of everything.

She started to stand, but he caught her hand. "Please ... give me five minutes."

She sat again.

He looked at her, his gaze never wavering. He licked his lips, took a breath, but remained silent as he watched her, and she looked down to break the unrelenting stare. She stroked her smoothie cup, rubbing her trembling fingers along the Styrofoam as he studied her. What was he looking for? Why was he staring at her that way, with such intensity? Had he just wanted to sit with her for five minutes? She squirmed a bit in the hard metal chair. He didn't relinquish the grip he had on her hand.

"My family is coming down for Thanksgiving," he finally said.

That was about the farthest thing from what she had expected him to say, and she looked up.

"My dad ... I told him what had happened. I told him about you, how great you are, how we had fought. I told him about your aunt and how we had figured out about his former relationship with your mom. That was a bit awkward because my mom was on the other line."

Jessica snickered before she could stop herself, probably more from nerves than anything.

"Anyway." He cleared his throat. "I'm inviting you to Thanksgiving dinner. You don't have to worry because my mom is cooking—not me. My dad wants to talk to you. He wants to tell you his side of the story."

Jessica chewed on her bottom lip for a second. "You want me to come?"

"Yes." He didn't hesitate a moment. "I would love for you to come."

Jessica fought back tears that were threatening to fall. After the way she had treated him the last few weeks, he hadn't given up ... instead, he had been looking for a way to help her find answers. She didn't want him to let go of her hand. She didn't want things to be awkward anymore. Could he feel the thrumming of her pulse under her skin, leaping from the joy that he actually wanted her to come over for Thanksgiving? Her elation ... it revealed to her a little something buried under the surface. She'd doubted the degree of his affection. Doubted his sincerity.

"Had you already made plans?"

"Not really." She shook her head. "Courtney said I could come over to her folks' place, but they never have turkey ... only ham. And Amber had invited me to go home with her but I didn't really want to."

"Speaking of Amber," Chad said, "could you pass on a message for me?"

Jessica braced herself. Why had she brought Amber up? Had Amber made any headway in her efforts while Jessica had been avoiding him? She couldn't bear to have this hope returned to her only to be taken away again.

"Could you let her know that while I think she's very sweet, I'm really not interested in her that way?" Chad's blue eyes held hers and bore straight to her soul.

Jessica's heart fluttered in her chest. "You're not?"

"You really have to ask that?" Chad reached over and tucked a strand of her hair back behind her ear. "I've been coming here every night for over a week to try and catch you because you avoid me like the plague at church. I'm sitting here not letting go of your hand for fear you're going to run away and I'll have to hunt you down all over again. I just invited you to spend Thanksgiving with my family. I honestly don't know what else to do."

Tears squeezed past Jessica's barriers and slid down her cheeks.

Chad moved to the chair next to her. "I'm sorry, Jessica. I'm sorry for this whole mess. I should have told you 'no' when you wanted to go with me to Arkansas and then we wouldn't be in this disaster."

"I didn't let you." She scooted closer to him.

"I didn't want to give up the thought of you and me for hours in the car just the two of us. So I could get to know you better. I loved the thought of having you there for me at the funeral. I wanted you to meet my family and have them meet you." He covered her hand with his other one.

"And I messed it all up."

"No." He squeezed her hand. "The past messed it all up."

She nodded, glad he hadn't said it was her aunt's fault. She still wasn't happy with Aunt Ruth, but she also didn't want him bringing that fight back up. That's what started them down this awkward road in the first place.

"Are you sleeping any better?" Chad brushed a tear from her cheek with his thumb.

Jessica shrugged. "Not much."

"I've been worried about you," he said softly. "It's like you're afraid to let yourself trust in God ... or in me."

Guilt gnawed at her. He had mentioned God the other day and she had pushed the question aside. In her angst over her dreams and the conflict with her aunt, she had completely forgotten about his concern over her faith. It was something she needed to work on. She just wasn't used to a guy who brought things like that up. Austin had been sweet, had attended worship services with her, but had never really talked about faith outside of the church building.

"I'll be okay." She was telling him as much as she was telling herself.

"Promise?"

"Promise."

He had leaned fairly close to her, his arm around the back of her seat and his chair pulled to almost touching hers. She was suddenly aware that a few other people were around, going in and out of the shop, eating on the other side of the windows. But when she glanced over at Chad, she couldn't move away. He studied her, concern written on his face.

"Can you do me a favor?" he asked.

"What?"

"My mom's birthday is next week, too. Can you help me pick something out to give her? I'm not good at shopping for women." He gave a little shrug.

She laughed. "Does she read?"

"Of course."

"Follow me to the bookstore and we'll find something there for her." Jessica stood up on shaky legs. She was still unsure about things, but maybe his dad would have more answers than the women in her family had offered. A tremulous sliver of hope started to glimmer inside. If Chad was willing to go to all the trouble of hunting her down and talking about his dad's past relationship with his mom on the phone, she had to be willing to at least explore the possibility that this might actually work out.

Chapter Fifteen

Jessica set the bells to ringing as she pushed through the door into the abandoned bookstore.

Courtney hollered from upstairs, "Is that you, Jessie?"

"Yes. I'm going to be down here a little while."

Chad followed her farther into the store. "It's weird to be in a store when it's closed."

"You get used to it." Jessica flipped on another light. "Now, does your mom like romances, cookbooks, histories, devotionals, sci fi?"

"I've seen her reading romance novels." Chad's fingers ran over a stack of books in the middle of the room. "Although a cookbook might be a neat idea, too. She's always talking about how she's tired of making the same old things she's always made."

"Well, the Christian romance section is here. We don't carry anything that's not clean so you don't have to worry about that. And the cookbooks are in the next room over on the shelf by the window." Jessica pointed to where she referred.

Courtney came downstairs. "Who are you talking to?"

Chad raised a hand in greeting.

"Well, hey stranger." Courtney raised an eyebrow at Jessica that said they would talk later, and went back upstairs.

"Does she approve of me?" Chad asked.

"It depends on how many more times she catches me crying." Jessica glanced at him.

Chad pulled her into his arms. "I never want to make you cry."

She relaxed into him and laid her head on his chest, catching a slight whiff of animals and antiseptic, a scent becoming more dear to her each day. His heart beat a steady rhythm under her ear. Everything seemed better here. All the bad stuff just disappeared. Slowly, he released her and took a step back.

"Guess I better find what I'm going to buy since you're actually closed," he said.

"Guess so." She nodded, missing his touch already.

Her phone rang and she jumped at the sudden disturbance of the quiet. He moved off to peruse bookshelves while she stepped over to the counter to answer her call.

"Hey, Jess," her mom said.

"Hey, Mom. What's up?"

"I just hadn't talked to you since that night right after your trip to Ruth's and I wanted to see how things were going."

"Better." Jessica perched on the stool. "They were bad for a while, but they're going better."

"I'm so glad. I was afraid you weren't ever going to talk to your aunt again from the way you sounded."

"I haven't talked to her." Jessica straightened a stack of bookmarks next to the register. "It's probably going to take me a long time to get back to where I feel like I can again. She said some pretty harsh things."

"Well, then you may not like what I'm about to tell you." Her mom took a deep breath. "It's her turn to host Christmas. We're all going there this year instead of to our house."

Jessica fiddled with a fake pumpkin that sat by the register. So many good memories ran through Jessica's head. Holidays at Aunt Ruth's house were almost a given. But she couldn't handle the thought of having Aunt Ruth ruin Christmas by making harsh comments about her boyfriend, either. "What if I just come and celebrate with you guys before or after you have it with her?"

"Jess, you know she's all alone and loves to share the holiday with our family. We're all she's got left."

"She'll still have you and Dad and Brittney." Jessica squeezed the bridge of her nose. "It's not like my absence is going to leave her completely alone."

"Jessica Ruth." Her mom pulled out her stern voice. "She is family and you will not treat her like this."

"What about how she treats me? She told me I wasn't allowed in her house as long as I was dating Chad."

Chad poked his head around the bookshelf and looked at her.

"She didn't really mean that."

"It sure sounded like she did." Jessica cringed at how whiny she sounded. "She doesn't want me there, Mom."

"I'll talk to her again," her mom said. "It will be fine."

"Did she even tell you how things really went down while I was up there?"

"I got her side of the story, if that's what you mean," her mom said. "It sounded a lot like yours."

Jessica leaned back against the cash register again. "And did she sound like she was sorry for it?"

Her mom paused and then said, "No."

"Until she is, I'm not going back there," Jessica said matter-of-factly. "Or until she gives me the reason that she feels the way she does about Chad's family."

"Jessica."

"No, Mom. No." Jessica shook her head even though her mom couldn't see it. "I will come to your house if you'll have me and I can bring your presents then, but I'm not going back in her house until I get one of those two things."

"I'll touch base with you later about it." Her mom sighed. "Maybe you'll change your mind."

Jessica watched Chad as he browsed cookbooks. "Don't count on it."

She ended her conversation with her mother badly, but she had little remorse over it. She wasn't going to let her aunt ruin again what she and Chad were tentatively putting back together. She walked over to where he flipped through a dessert book.

"I thought you said she wanted one so she could have more options instead of making the same thing over and over. That one is just desserts." She giggled, wondering how much he had overheard.

"And you don't think people need variety in desserts, too?" He set the book back on the shelf and handed her another one he had set to the side. "I like this one."

"I'll ring it up for you." Jessica started walking to the counter. "Do we need to wrap it, too?"

"Jess." His voice sounded so serious that she stopped and turned around. "What were you and your mom talking about?"

She looked down at the cookbook and flipped it over in her hands as she tried to come up with what to say.

"Am I causing you more trouble?" he asked.

"No!" Jessica looked up in shock.

"Really? Because it sounds like you just had a fight with your mom over me."

Jessica started toward the cash register again. "We were just starting to make Christmas plans."

"At your aunt Ruth's?" he asked.

"It's her year to host." Jessica laid the book on the counter with a sigh. "Mom told me I should come. I said 'no.'"

He put his hands over hers as she started to add up his purchase. "I don't want to come between you and your family."

"It's her fault, not yours. She's the one who ostracized me." She pulled her hand away. "I really shouldn't even charge you for this since you covered all of Lester's costs."

"How is he?" Chad leaned his elbows on the counter.

"He's good. He's gotten even friskier as the weather has cooled a bit this last week. He likes to dash around the apartment right under our feet in the mornings. Courtney's about to kick him out, I think."

"It was my pleasure to take care of him," he said. "Besides, I told you what I'd accept as payment and you turned me down."

Jessica licked her lips and met his eyes. "I'm such a mess, Chad. What do you even see in me?"

He reached over and brushed a piece of hair behind her ear. "Besides the fact that you're beautiful?"

She ducked her head.

"You're a wonderful Christian. You care about people and want to take their pain away. You want to remain pure for God and your future husband. You laugh at my jokes. You love cats. Want me to keep going?"

She shook her head. "I've been horrible to you for two weeks now. And yet, you hunted me down and invited me to dinner. You compliment me and act like I'm the best thing in the world. I'm just a person—and one with a lot more baggage than she wants to have."

"I don't think your aunt would appreciate being called baggage." He gave her a half-grin.

She smiled in return. "She wouldn't."

"Ring me up and I'll leave you alone for tonight." He got out his wallet. "May I sit with you again on Sunday?"

"That's probably the easiest way to tell Amber you're not interested in her." Jessica gave him a cocky smile.

He paid for the book and let her wrap it in shiny blue paper, paper that perfectly matched his eyes. Then, on top, she tied white ribbon and curled it into tight ringlets.

"Almost as pretty as you are." He fingered the bow. "Thanks for letting me come shop after hours."

She looked up at him. "Thanks for finding me."

"I had to. I was starting to have nightmares of never seeing you again." He ran his hand over her cheek, then leaned over and kissed her forehead. "Now maybe both of us will have a good night's sleep."

He slipped out the back door and she latched it behind him. She walked slowly up the stairs and faced her curious roommate waiting for her on the couch.

"I guess you can tell Amber for sure that Chad's not interested in her." Jessica gave her a grin.

"I already told her he wouldn't be." Courtney shook her head. "Who could get over someone like you that fast?"

"You been taking lessons from Chad on sweet talk?" Jessica grabbed a pint of ice cream out of the freezer and two spoons from the drawer. She tossed one spoon to her roommate and plopped down on the other end of the couch. Her cat looked up sleepily from his spot in the middle and then lowered his head and went back to sleep.

"So, spill." Courtney took a huge spoonful of mint chocolate chip ice cream. "I want to know all the way back to Halloween. You've been holding out on me."

Jessica laughed and swallowed her own bite of dessert. "Yes, ma'am."

Jessica and Courtney stayed up late into the night as Jessica relayed to her best friend all that had been going on. She told about the fight, about the trip to Chad's clinic, about the fact that he just showed up at the smoothie shop tonight. And she brought up the fact that Chad questioned her faith.

"I sort of agree." Courtney gave Jessica a thoughtful look.

"So what do I do to change that? How do I trust again?"

"Have you forgiven Austin?"

Jessica sighed and leaned back against the arm of the couch.

"You can't move on until you relinquish the past. Austin wasn't necessarily the best boyfriend, but you had some good times with him. I think you forgot that in your disappointment of his life choices at the end. But you're supposed to be a Christian. And God wants us all to forgive others. I think it would be a big step in the right direction."

Jessica nodded. Forgive Austin? She had built so many hopes on him when they were together, only to have them crushed in the end. Would offering him forgiveness finally release her from that disappointment and fear? Would it help her trust again, like Courtney had suggested? Jessica's breath caught in her throat ... would she have to talk to him to really, truly forgive him?

"So you and Chad are good again?" Courtney asked.

"We're getting there." Jessica leaned forward. "I really want this to work."

"I really want it to work for you. So, no more fighting. I can't stand living with a zombie." Courtney pointed her spoon at Jessica.

"If we don't go to bed soon, we're both going to be zombies." Jessica grabbed the spoon from her friend and took them to the kitchen.

The girls went to their separate rooms, Lester following Jessica into hers. He hopped up onto her bed and made a nest before curling up right in the center. Leaning over her desk, Jessica shook her head and clicked to check her email one more time before she joined him.

She selected her inbox to see what new emails had appeared over the last few hours. She sat down in the chair with a thump. Her finger shook as she hit the button on her laptop to open the email ... from Austin Vasquez. She wondered at the coincidence after her earlier conversation.

Jessie, Let me just say that you were right and I was wrong. Three months ago when you told me "no," you were only doing what was right. I want to apologize for putting you through that. These last few months have been so lonely for me. I wanted to tell you that you're the best thing that ever happened to me. I still don't know what my life is going to be like without your ray of sunshine lighting it up. I miss you, Jess. Can you ever forgive me?

Chapter Sixteen

Jessica closed Austin's email without answering it. What was he hoping for when he sent it? Reconciliation? She didn't want to have anything to do with him. A little voice in her head chided her, reminding her that she had agreed to try and forgive him. "I will forgive him. But I'm dating Chad now and Austin can stay in the past," she told herself. However, as if her dreams were schizophrenic, both boys continued to play major roles in her nightly visions.

Thanksgiving morning she followed the directions Chad had given her. He lived in a newer neighborhood in Honey Springs, where the homes were good-sized and the yards were smaller. As she pulled up to the address he had scribbled across the bulletin on Sunday morning, she had to look again to make sure it was right. The house was lovely with a red-brick exterior and white stone accents on the corners and around the windows and garage doors. It was a two story and she could see a chandelier through the window above the front door. She parked next to the curb and shook her head. *He lives in a place like this and I invited him to our run-down apartment? What must he think of me?*

A woman with light brown hair answered the door with a smile, "Jessica?"

"Yes." Jessica gave a nod, vaguely remembering seeing her with Chad back at the funeral.

"I'm Marla, Chad's mom." She opened the door wider, releasing the tantalizing aroma of roasting turkey. "Come on in. I think everyone's still in the den watching the parade."

Jessica followed her through the foyer along a gorgeous cherry-wood staircase to the right and down the hallway past the kitchen and into the den. Two large sofas filled most of the space and faced a flat-screen television hung over a warm fireplace. Chad jumped up as she walked into the room.

"I didn't even hear the doorbell."

"That's okay." Marla patted his arm. "I let her in."

"Thanks, Mom." Chad leaned down and kissed her on the forehead before coming over to give Jessica a hug. "Any problems finding it?"

"Nope," Jessica said into his chest.

"This is my sister, Gabby." Chad pointed to the brunette a little younger than they were who sat on the couch and watched them with eyes the same blue as Chad's. Again, Jessica remembered seeing her in Arkansas.

"Gabriella, actually." She waved her hand at her brother. "Chad's the only one who calls me Gabby."

Jessica smiled at her.

"And you've met my dad." Chad motioned to the other end of the sofa.

Jessica nodded.

"Want to see the rest of the house?" Chad asked as she glanced around the room.

"Sure." Was the sky blue? Of course she did. A tour of the house might give her more insights into this man she hadn't quite figured out yet.

Curiosity warred with jealousy as they climbed the stairs. The hallway branched off into two bedrooms on the right, both with signs of life only in the air mattresses and suitcases that were obviously being used by his parents and sister. No other furniture or artwork gave any indication that the rooms were ever used. What held him back from buying furniture and decorating? Money? Time? Was he waiting for a wife? Children? Whoa! Where did that thought come from? And why did she like the idea so much of being included in it? The front bedroom was above the dining room and had a bay window that would be just perfect for a window seat and a good book. She knew exactly what color she would want the cushion to be. She shook her head to try and loosen the image ... this wasn't her house. And as shaky as things had been, she had absolutely no right to think it might be one day in the future.

Downstairs, the dining room table was already set for the feast with bright orange plates and leaf-printed napkins. The office was done in masculine tones, with books lining one wall and a heavy wooden desk right in the middle. The spacious kitchen where his mom was putting together the dressing was the last stop. A breakfast nook was between the kitchen and the den.

Jessica had a room and a bathroom over the bookstore, and he had a house that would fit a family of five or six. "Your house is so nice, Chad. You must think our place is a dump." She leaned back against the island.

"Are you kidding?" Chad snatched a bite of apple out of the bowl of fruit salad on the counter. "I love your place. It's got character. I really wanted an older house with a bigger yard. But this one was such a good deal, I went ahead and bought it. Figured I could find something else later, once I had my practice established. I just haven't bothered to take the time to look yet."

"This house needs a woman's touch." Marla waved her knife around, almost catching it in the silky scarf artfully tied around her neck. "It's a fine house, but it looks like a man lives here."

"A man does live here." Chad straightened to his full height.

A fat gray striped cat walked through the kitchen and wound its way between Jessica's legs. She reached down to rub his head, and he purred and leaned into her hand. She scratched under his ears and he rolled over on his back to give her access to his belly.

"Well, Rufus sure seems to like you." Chad leaned over to pet him, too.

"Rufus likes anyone who will love on him." Marla snuck her own bite of fruit with a wink. "He's a spoiled old thing."

"How old is he?" Jessica asked.

Chad silently ticked off years on his fingers before he answered. "I'd say around twelve. I got him when I was about sixteen, I think."

"Wow," Jessica said.

"When Chad moved in here, we brought Rufus down." Marla reached over to tenderly touch Chad's cheek for a moment, her brown eyes sparkling with affection. "Rob's not really an animal person, but we kept the cat for Chad while he was in school. Rob was very happy to be able to kick him out of our house."

"He's completely spoiled and thinks he runs the house." Chad stood back up. "But he's a good cat. And he's getting old. He has trouble with the stairs so mostly he just hangs out down here."

"If you guys will get out of my hair, dinner would get done sooner." Marla pointed a banana at Chad in a teasing manner to shoo them out of the kitchen.

"Is there anything I can do to help?" Jessica asked.

Marla glanced around the kitchen, as if a task would leap into the air. "No. I have everything under control."

"Does she hate me because I'm Sandy's daughter?" Jessica whispered to Chad as they walked back into the den.

"Don't be silly." Chad put his arm around her shoulders. "She's just busy with lunch, and she takes a while to warm up to. I think she's sort of watching you today to see if you're worthy of her son."

"No pressure there," Jessica said under her breath.

"No worries." He gave her a squeeze. "You're totally worthy."

Jessica decided to ignore that comment.

"I'm surprised you don't have a dog." Jessica sat down on the couch between Chad and Gabriella.

"Dogs take a lot more work than cats do." Chad shrugged. "I didn't think it'd be fair if I didn't have much time to give it any attention."

"Plus his yard is the size of a postage stamp." Rob held his hands up only about a foot apart.

"It's not that bad." Chad tossed a pillow at his dad. "But a dog would probably appreciate having more room to romp around."

"Yeah, to get a dog to fit the size of your yard, Chad, you'd have to get something disgusting like a Chihuahua." Gabriella wrinkled her freckled nose.

Chad stuck his tongue out at her.

The announcers on the television described one of the floats, a large contraption of different pilgrim and Native American heads that turned back and forth. Everyone there was dressed warmly for the chilly New York weather. In Austin it was supposed to be in the upper sixties. Jessica was still getting used to Texas weather versus the northern Arkansas weather she had grown up with. Autumn in Texas seemed to only last about a week before all the leaves were gone and winter was blowing in.

She glanced over and caught Rob looking her way, his eyes almost the exact same shade as Chad's.

"Sorry." He gave her a sheepish smile. "You just look so much like your mom."

"I have my dad's eyes." Jessica opened them as wide as they would go.

Rob chuckled and turned his attention back to the screen. The fireplace popped and crackled under the sound of the marching bands in the parade. Clanks and gurgles came from Marla working in the kitchen. Rufus put his paws up on the edge of the couch and Chad gently lifted the old cat up where he could snuggle between them. She rubbed the cat's head and accidently brushed against Chad's hand as he reached to do the same thing. He caught her hand in his and didn't let go. Unlike the other night at the smoothie shop, it wasn't a grip to keep her from running away. Instead, this was warm and comfortable, and a peace she hadn't even realized was missing seemed to slip into place inside her heart.

Marla called them all in to eat a little after twelve. Jessica followed Chad into the formal dining room and took her seat at the gorgeous oak table. It was the kind of table that could expand to hold a huge family, the kind she hoped to have one day. The family held hands as Rob led them in prayer, and Chad gave Jessica's an extra squeeze when they said "amen."

"I want to apologize for the dishes we're using." Marla passed the turkey platter. "If I had known that Chad only had four place-settings, I would have brought some of mine so we wouldn't have to use these paper things."

"It'll just make it easier to do the dishes." Jessica took a helping of sweet potato casserole piled high with brown sugar and marshmallows.

"Well, I just wanted to make sure you knew our family didn't usually do paper plates at holidays." Marla passed the green bean casserole.

"It tastes just as good on paper as it does on real plates, Mom. Stop fretting about it." Chad whipped his napkin out and spread it in his lap as if it were cloth.

Rob took a large slice of turkey and looked at Jessica. "After we eat, maybe you and I will take a walk to that park down the street and we can talk."

Marla's mouth tightened.

Jessica gave a quick nod. "Sure."

"Mind if I tag along?" Chad touched her back as he passed the gravy. "I need to be able to eat everything I want and still have room for pumpkin pie later. I figure it'll help if I take a walk."

Gabriella rolled her eyes. "You're such a dork."

"Love you, too, Gabby." Chad grabbed a roll out of the basket and wiggled his eyebrows at his sister.

Jessica couldn't help but smile. Gabriella reminded Jessica of her own sister.

"So, Jessica." Marla took a sip of tea. "Chad says you have a bookstore."

Jessica swallowed the bite in her mouth. "My roommate and I run a little one downtown. We both love books so much it's sometimes hard to sell them instead of just reading them all."

"Do you have any new ones in the 'God's Little Mysteries' series?" Marla carefully cut a piece of meat.

"I think I saw one come in the other day. I'll try to remember to set it back for you if you're interested."

Marla nodded before Rob took over the questions. "You said you run it with your roommate? Where did you go to school?"

"Harding University." Jessica wondered if she should set her fork down until Chad's parents were finished with their questions.

"That's where your mom graduated from, too, right?" Rob mopped up some gravy with his roll.

She cut a glance over at Marla. Jessica had no desire to tick Chad's mom off by talking about Rob's ex-fiancée. "It is."

"And your family ... they're all doing well?" Rob evidently hadn't noticed Jessica's hesitation.

"Yes. My sister is going to graduate in the spring. I think my parents are trying to figure out what they'll do as empty nesters."

"How's your school going, Gabby?" Chad rescued Jessica from any more questions. She shot him a grateful smile.

All too soon the turkey, cornbread dressing, sweet potatoes, green beans and rolls were eaten to the point that no one felt they could take another bite. They sat for a few moments, sipping sweet tea and enjoying the feeling of being full. Then, Marla got up to clear the dishes and Jessica jumped up to help.

"You can just leave that there." Marla said as Jessica grabbed a casserole dish.

"It's no trouble." Jessica followed her into the kitchen.

"You really don't have to help." Marla brushed a lock of her shoulder-length brown hair back and rolled up the sleeves of her cardigan. "Like you pointed out, it shouldn't take that long since we ate on paper plates."

"I was raised to help with the dishes when someone has me over for dinner." Jessica stuffed a paper plate in the trash can.

Marla scraped turkey scraps and some gravy into a dish and put it down for Rufus who was begging at her feet. "Well, thank you then." She scraped the rest of the gravy into a plastic container.

"You're welcome." Jessica returned to the dining room to get some more dishes.

"You're making us look bad." Chad followed her back into the kitchen with two dishes in his own hands. "Mom's going to expect us to help from now on."

"It'll be good for you."

Marla glanced up with a smile.

Rob came in as they finished loading the dishwasher and waited for Jessica and Chad to grab their jackets. Then, they all headed out into the fall afternoon. Leaves crunched under their feet as they walked down the sidewalk. Immaculately kept grass and neat flowerbeds graced almost every yard they passed. Rob didn't say anything until they were at the park two blocks from Chad's house. Jessica studied the back of Chad's father as they walked. Would he reveal who had come between him and her mom? Did he know why Aunt Ruth was so set against their family? They turned onto the walking trail and followed it until they came to a bench.

Rob took one end. He seemed at ease despite the pending conversation. How could he remain so calm? But Chad was the same way. The only time Jessica had really seen Chad get upset was Halloween night. Chad and Rob also shared a similar stature, held themselves in the same way. Jessica could imagine what Chad would look like in thirty years and she didn't mind it. Except for a slight paunch and some silver mixed in with his brown hair, he and Chad could have been brothers.

Jessica and Chad sat down on the other end. Chad's arm draped over the back around Jessica's shoulders, and she reveled in the comfort of his strength. Despite the beautiful weather, the park remained fairly abandoned. A playground a few feet farther down the trail only had one occupied swing. This part of the trail was surrounded mostly by bushes, shrubs, and flowers giving their last hurrah before cold weather. There wasn't much to distract Jessica from the reason they were there.

Rob took a deep breath and stared off into the distance.

Jessica squirmed a bit as she waited for him to start. Was he still in love with her mom? Maybe she should never have agreed to have this conversation. She didn't want to bring up something that could ruin Chad's family. Maybe she should just tell him she didn't want to know after all. Things weren't so bad now, were they? Except for her relationship issues with Aunt Ruth ...

"Chad said you know I was engaged to your mom for a while." Rob glanced her way.

Jessica nodded.

"Did your mom tell you why we ended it?"

Jessica shook her head. "She just said that someone came between you two."

"That's one way to put it." Rob gave a bitter laugh.

"So what does that mean, Dad?" Chad pulled Jessica in closer to him.

Rob's eyes searched the distance again, as if watching a film of his past against the blue car parked across the street. "We started off okay when we began dating ... at least I thought we did. Your mom—and when I look at you,

Jessica, I can't help but think of how she looked that first day we met—she was completely enamored with me, and it didn't take her long to make me believe I felt the same toward her."

Jessica smiled, picturing her high-spirited, loving, see-no-evil mom as a spunky teenager, crushing on a boy who looked a lot like Chad. Even though she had first rebelled against the idea of her mom being in love with someone other than her dad, now that she knew the Mannings, it wasn't hard to see why she had been.

"We dated for two years before I asked her to marry me. By that time, I knew without a doubt that her sister wasn't thrilled with the thought of our relationship." Rob looked at Chad and Jessica. "I hear she hasn't changed much."

Jessica shook her head.

Rob nodded and went on. "I was stupid and thought we could work through whatever Ruth had against us. So, onward we plowed, but the closer we got to the wedding, the worse it got."

"The worse what got?" Chad asked.

"Ruth and Sandy's relationship. They couldn't spend two minutes in a room together without fighting. I ended up drying my fiancée's tears more than helping with wedding plans."

~1980~

"It's just two weeks to the wedding." Rob drove Sandy home at the end of a date.

"I wish it were tonight. I don't want to have to live in the same house with Ruth anymore."

Sandy leaned her head against the window of the car as they cruised down her street.

"It hasn't gotten any better, has it?" Rob asked. "Think we can figure out what she's so upset about?"

"No." Sandy shook her head. "I don't think I ever will. I've tried so many times."

Rob parked in front of Sandy's house and turned the car off. The neighborhood was quiet, and streetlights shadowed their faces so it was hard for him to make out her expression. He turned toward Sandy and took her hands in his. "Sandy, are you sure you want to go through with this?"

"With what, Rob?"

"With our wedding."

Sandy froze, a look of terror on her face. "What are you talking about?"

"I'm talking about the fact that if you marry me you may never have a relationship with your sister again." Rob let his head fall back against the headrest with a quiet thud that practically echoed against the growing pain in his heart. This was the farthest thing from what he wanted, but he couldn't come up with a better solution no matter how hard he tried. "I don't want to do that to you."

"I'm marrying you, Rob." Sandy shook her head adamantly, the swishing of her brown ponytail emphasizing each shake. "I don't care what Ruth thinks."

"Yes, you do." He intertwined his fingers with hers, pressing their palms together. "Every time she says something to you about me, you end up fighting with her, crying, sad. I don't want that to go on for the rest of our lives. We're going to see her every Christmas, on holidays, whenever we visit your family. What if she never gets over this? What if she holds this against you forever?"

"We're getting married in two weeks!" Sandy's voice squeaked at the end. Her grasp on his hands tightened and he hid a cringe as some of her nails bit into his skin.

"Nothing is set in stone until we say 'I do.'" Rob shifted so that his leg wasn't pressed against the gear shift. "We don't have to break up completely, but we could just step back a little and put this on hold for a while until you can work it out with your sister."

"But I don't want to step back," Sandy whispered. Her bottom lip trembled and she blinked, loosening some of the moisture that clung to her lashes.

"I don't, either." Rob pulled a hand away to tuck a loose strand of hair behind her ear. "But I can't stand to see you so sad."

Tears ran down her face, but this time it was Rob's fault instead of Ruth's. She shook her head, and pulled her hands away to wipe at her cheeks.

"How are we going to let everyone know that it's postponed? We've already got everything scheduled and ordered. What about the deposits we put down on the building and the rentals and everything else?" Sandy's voice was close to hysteria.

"Hey." Rob put his hand on her shoulder and leaned forward to look into her eyes. He hated this! He was trying to be the voice of reason, to figure out a way to make things better, and instead seemed to just be messing them up more. "Our family and friends will help. You know your mom has been worried about you lately, just like I have. It'll work out."

"Do I still call you my fiancé?" she asked and played with the ring on her finger.

"I guess not for now." Another stab to his heart. Could Ruth really do more harm to their relationship down the road than he was doing tonight? "Even though you and I know we want to get married, maybe if we don't make such a big deal out of it, Ruth will open up to you enough that you can figure out what's going on."

Sandy slowly slid the diamond off her hand and held it out to Rob. "I can still see you, though, right?"

"I couldn't stand it if you didn't." He gave her a small smile as he reluctantly accepted the jewelry. He had agonized over this ring, trying to find the cut and style that would suit her the best. He had scrimped and saved, knowing it would all be worth it when her eyes lit up brighter than the stone. How could he stand to have her walk around without it on her finger? It told the world that this was his girl.

"I guess there's nothing else to say tonight, then." She nodded, leaned forward and kissed his cheek. "I'll love you forever."

It sounded so final. He closed his eyes and breathed in the floral scent of her perfume as she lingered a moment longer, her soft skin pressed against his. He watched her climb out of the car and slowly walk up the sidewalk, her back giving nothing away as she mounted the steps and entered the house. Had he just made the biggest mistake of his life? Why wasn't he running after her, beating on the door? His heart was in his throat and he didn't even notice the diamond cutting into his clenched palm.

Chapter Seventeen

Ruth didn't say anything when Sandy made her announcement, but Sandy could have sworn that she saw her sister hastily cover a gloat. Their mom wrapped Sandy in her arms and held her while she cried. Their father just shook his head and started making a list of people to call.

It was all hands on deck to undo all the plans Sandy and Rob had meticulously made over the past year. Sandy looked across the table at Ruth as they sat going through the list of wedding gifts and deciding what needed to be returned versus just stored away for a later date. Ruth tapped her pencil against her page of silverware, towels and vases, but didn't seem any happier or different at all. The only real difference Sandy could see in her sister was the fact that now that the wedding plans were being reversed, Ruth no longer fought against every decision or request for help.

Had she and Rob split up for no reason? Had they just given in to what Ruth expected and seemed to want to happen instead of trying to prove that she was wrong? Had it really been worth it just to have her sister no longer refusing to help? Sandy would have moved out in a couple weeks and not had to deal with it anymore. She choked back the seemingly constant lump in her throat and tried to refocus on the task at hand. What was she going to do with a crystal punch bowl set when she wasn't even going to have her own home yet?

She saw Rob at church several days later, but he didn't sit with her like usual. Even though they had agreed to see each other still, he stuck to his promise to keep from making a big deal out of their relationship around Ruth. Sandy chose to ignore Ruth's raised eyebrow. Instead, she traced the spot on her finger where his diamond ring should have been and promised herself that they would find a way to get it back there.

Two weeks continued that way, and the date of the wedding came ... and went. Sandy spent the day locked in her room. She had no desire whatsoever to see anyone who might show her sympathy ... or even not show her sympathy.

The summer was almost over when her dad came up to her and handed her a piece of paper. She unfolded it and read the top line. Then, she read it again.

"You want me to go somewhere else to school?" Sandy asked.

"I know you've enjoyed going to the junior college in the next town over, but your mother and I think that with everything that has happened between you and Rob, maybe it's time for you to expand your horizons a bit. Plus, we thought it might be easier if you didn't have to see him every day."

"Dad, I told you, Rob and I are still a couple. We're just putting off getting married for a while." Sandy went to hand the paper back to him, but he didn't take it.

"That's what you said, but from what I can see you haven't spoken to Rob Manning in over four weeks."

"We're taking a break, Dad. He's the only guy I've ever dated, and we decided we should take a breath before taking such a big step as getting married." Sandy waved the hand that still felt naked without Rob's ring. "But we're still a couple."

"Sandy, it won't hurt you while you're waiting for this breath to be over to go to a better school than the one you had settled for so you could be with Rob. I know he's a great guy, but until you figure out what's going on, here is another option. Just think about it." He left her standing in the hallway.

Her mom was the only person she told the true reason that she and Rob had separated for a while. The evening after her father had suggested a different school, she joined her mom on the front porch swing and snuggled in close like she had done her whole life. With tears and a few outbursts, she admitted how much Ruth had played a part in the summer's events.

"I hated to see you and Ruth at odds with each other. I wish I knew what issue she has with him, but she won't talk to me, either." Her mom shook her head. "The only thing I can remember is that she hasn't ever been the same since she came home from college. Sometimes, I wish there weren't six years between the two of you. I think you could have gotten along better if you were closer in age."

Sandy sighed. "Do you really think me going to Harding University to finish up college is the best idea?"

Her mom shrugged. "I'm not sure of anything anymore, but I trust your father. His judgment has always led us right. And God's. 'Trust in Jehovah with all thy heart, and lean not upon thine own understanding.'"

Sandy finished quoting the Bible verse with her mother, "In all thy ways acknowledge him, and he will direct thy paths."

"It's true." Her mom squeezed her hand. "Go pray about it, Honey. God will show you what to do."

Two and a half weeks later, Sandy left for Harding. She had not talked to Rob again since their last discussion, the night they called off the wedding.

~2011~

"You didn't talk to her ever again?" Jessica asked Rob.

He leaned forward, resting his elbows on his knees. "No. Every time I called their house, Ruth answered. I even tried varying the times that I called. It was like she was answering every phone call that came in during those weeks. And Sandy never called me."

"But you were members of the same congregation." Jessica frowned in confusion.

"You sound like you wish we had gotten back together." Rob smiled.

She shook her head. "I'm just trying to figure out how it all happened."

"I didn't go up to her at church because Ruth was always right beside her. And much as I tried to motion to her to meet me afterwards to talk away from Ruth, she never seemed to see me."

Rob stood up and stretched. Jessica glanced at Chad and then back at his dad.

"When she left for a different school, I continued going to the local junior college. She met her husband and I met my wife. We moved on. We both love our spouses. I don't regret who I married and I assume the same for her. It's in the past." He pointed at the two of them. "But maybe you can find a way to make this the last generation that Ruth keeps from their first love." Rob gave a little nod. "I'll see you guys back at the house."

The sun warmed Jessica's head as she stared out over the yellowing grass and orange-leafed trees. They became a blur, just like her emotions. No one else was taking advantage of the warm holiday to enjoy the park so they had it to themselves. She leaned back against the bench and felt Chad's arm against her back. "What do you think?"

"About?" Chad asked.

"Your dad and my mom. They were so in love and then Aunt Ruth tore them apart. What if we're like that? What if we end up letting this whole situation break us up? I didn't talk to you for two weeks because of it. What if you hadn't found me at Smoothie Heaven that night?"

"My mom wouldn't have gotten a really great birthday present."

She eyed him.

One side of his mouth went up in a grin. He leaned forward and rested his elbows on his knees, just like she'd seen Rob do earlier. "Jess, we're not going to let it happen. We're trying to figure out what went wrong with them so it doesn't go wrong with us. Besides, think about it. If our parents hadn't broken up, we wouldn't even be here right now. You're half your mom, but you're also half your dad. If your mom had married my dad, she never would have had you. She would have had someone half me and half you." He cocked his head to the side as if he were trying to picture what someone like that would look like.

"The whole situation is messed up." Jessica ran a hand through her hair. "Somehow, something hurt my aunt in the past, and so she hurt my mom and your dad, and now she's hurting us. Mom thought Aunt Ruth was upset because Mom was younger and getting married first. But Mom still got married first because Aunt Ruth never got married."

"So we know it's not that your mom got married first." Chad checked it off on his finger.

"So we have to go back and figure out what happened to Aunt Ruth. Find out what made her this way."

"Might mean you have to face seeing her at Christmas." Chad cocked an eyebrow.

Jessica leaned her head back and stared up at the wispy clouds in the sky. "What if I can't?"

"I can do all things through Christ who strengthens me," Chad quoted from Philippians.

Jessica glanced over at him and sighed.

"Okay, so maybe it doesn't feel like it's much help when you're trying to face family, but it's true." Chad held his hands up in concession.

"This is so wrong." Jessica let out a puff of air. "I normally look forward to the holidays, to seeing my family. I loved getting to spend time with my aunt Ruth when I was growing up. Now, I'm dreading seeing her. How could things turn around so quickly?"

"But in some ways it hasn't been quick. This is something that's been building for over twenty years." Chad shifted to where he faced her. "It just feels fast to us because we jumped into the middle of the story. But for your aunt, it's been going on for a long time."

"It sort of stinks to not know the beginning of the story."

"So, we need to find out what the beginning is." Chad drew a circle in the air, as if he were rewinding a clock.

"It sounds like you're wanting to go to Sassafras with me over Christmas." Jessica sat up straighter and looked him squarely in the eye. "I'm pretty sure my aunt, while she told my mom I was welcome, would not welcome you under her roof."

"We haven't sold my grandfather's house yet. My parents are planning to spend the next week up there cleaning it out so they can, but it's still ours, officially. I'd have a place to stay if you want me to come."

"But you should spend Christmas with your family." Jessica leaned forward with her elbows on her knees.

"We could split it. Spend a few days with yours and a few days with mine," Chad said.

"We aren't married."

"I know, but if you're going to push me to spend time with my family as well as yours, that's the best suggestion I could come up with. And I really feel that you need to figure out what's going on with your aunt."

"I know I do." Jessica tucked a strand of hair behind her ear. "I just wish there were an easier way."

"Come on. Let's walk back to the house and watch football." Chad stood up and pulled her to join him.

"Football ... fun ..." Jessica said in a monotone.

"Or maybe my family will want to play a board game and you can get out of football." He playfully bumped his hip into hers.

She pushed him back and laughed. He grabbed her hand and swung it back and forth as they walked back to his house. A family several doors from Chad's home was hanging up their Christmas lights.

"Are you going to put lights up?" Jessica asked, nodding to the family.

"Hm. I hadn't really thought about it." Chad turned to look at the decorations more closely as if to see what they were supposed to look like. "I've never really had a tree or anything before. With it just being me, I figured it didn't matter that much. I always get to enjoy the one at my folks'."

"With a house like yours, you should put up lights." Jessica nodded.

"Today?" He laughed.

"Soon." She gave him a grin. "I love Christmas lights. We used to drive around and look at all the lights in the area and sing Christmas carols on Christmas Eve every year. I always thought I'd grow up and decorate my place with as many lights as I possibly could."

"You know what your electric bill would be like if you did that?"

"Wow." Jessica swatted him in the arm. "Way to be a mood killer."

He grinned at her. "Want to help me put some up tomorrow?"

She smiled in return. "Maybe."

Gabriella stuck her head out the front door and hollered at them. "Are you two love birds going to stay out there forever or do you want some of this pie?"

Jessica and Chad laughed and ran up the sidewalk to eat pie and play board games. There would be time later to face the issues standing against them.

Chapter Eighteen

Jessica heard her roommate come in later that night. Courtney stuck her head in the bedroom door a few minutes later. "You look like you had a great day."

Jessica turned her chair away from the computer to smile. "I did have a great day. I beat all the Mannings at Monopoly."

"Well, that's a good way to befriend your boyfriend's family." Courtney rolled her eyes.

"How was your day?"

"Nice." Courtney flopped on the bed. "My brothers both came down for the weekend, but I'm just as glad I don't have to sleep there, too. I love them, but I love them more from a distance."

"I know exactly what you mean." Jessica grinned.

"So, how goes the solving of the mystery?" Courtney asked. "Did his dad tell you all you needed to know?"

"No." Jessica sighed and tapped a pencil against her jeans. "I mean, he filled in some of the gaps, but we still can't figure out Aunt Ruth. And, by the way, she seems to be the cause of my mom and his dad breaking up."

"No surprise there." Courtney leaned back against the headboard.

Jessica shot her a dirty look. "But we still can't figure out why, and that's the point."

Courtney tapped a finger against her lips as she thought. "So, what's the plan?"

Jessica crossed her legs in the chair, disturbing Lester who had been asleep on her feet. "I guess I'll go to Christmas after all. That should make my mom happy, right?"

"So you haven't told her that plan, yet?"

"No." Jessica shook her head. "I haven't talked to her since the other day when she called to let me know it would be at Aunt Ruth's house."

"It'll work out. It's Christmas. She can't hold a grudge at Christmas, right?"

"You'd think." Jessica cocked an eyebrow. "She's held a grudge for how many years now?"

"Got plans for tomorrow night? Mom invited you over for leftovers." Courtney stood up again.

"Not sure yet. Chad mentioned maybe putting up Christmas lights, but I really don't think he owns any yet anyway, so probably not. I know I won't be doing any shopping. I despise Black Friday. Plus, we'll be working here most of the day."

"True. Well, think about it and let me know in the morning." Courtney paused in the doorway. "I'm headed to bed."

"Okay. Good night." Jessica turned back to her computer as a new email popped up. She clicked it open.

"Jessica, did you get my last email? I'd really like to talk to you," Austin wrote.

Jessica hit delete and turned off her monitor. She rubbed Lester's head and then got ready for bed. Tomorrow would be a long day, and she didn't need to think about that person anymore.

***

The girls really didn't expect a rush of people to come through the store, even though it was Black Friday, but they were ready just in case. Jessica took down the fall decorations. Didn't she just put these up? After putting those away, she dug through boxes to find Christmas ones while Courtney covered the cash register during the morning. Several families came in and browsed as she emerged from the storage room with a string of plastic holly leaves around her neck. Jessica smiled at the sound of the kids playing in the children's room of the store.

The bells jingled on the door. Another customer. Maybe the Christmas season really was helping business. Jessica continued to hang the garland on the staircase. She hummed along with the easy listening station playing on their speaker system.

As she backed down the stairs, wrapping the garland as she went along, a pair of hands covered her eyes. She froze, lifting her fingers to cover them, trying to figure out who they belonged to.

"Ho, ho, ho," a voice whispered in her ear.

"Chad." She couldn't help but grin as she turned around to see him.

"Thought you could use a wreath for your front door." He pointed to the greenery still beside the entryway. "Got a wreath holder?"

"I'll go find it in the back room." She hopped off the bottom step.

"My mom liked her cookbook so much that she decided to come with me to look for another one." Chad motioned over his shoulder to where Marla browsed in front of a bookshelf. "I'll just hang out with her until you get back."

"Great." She thumbed in the direction she was headed. "Be right back."

She pushed into the storeroom and stepped around the boxes of pumpkins, leaves, and cornucopias to get back to the corner of other decorations. She scooted several tubs of Easter eggs and garlands out of the way to find a box of random miscellany. The door jingled again as she opened that box and dug through suction cups, fishing line, and sticky tack.

She finally found the metal wreath holder in the bottom of the box, tangled in old Christmas ornament hooks and an unwound spool of striped ribbon. She pulled it out and started back toward the front of the store. As she got to the doorway, Courtney shouted, "Get out!"

Jessica stopped just before the entrance of the store.

What in the world?

"No. She doesn't want to see you. I want you out of this store now," Courtney said, her voice firm.

Jessica inched forward so she could see the cash register and Courtney. In front of the counter stood a man with thick blond hair and wide shoulders. She didn't have to see the man's face to know who it was. He motioned to Courtney as he spoke, his voice low and composed. The other voices in the store had gone quiet.

"I have to talk to her. I know she's around. Just tell me where she is." Austin held his hands up. "I'll have a chat with her, and then I'll leave." Jessica took another step forward. She had forgotten how calm his voice could be. When they had broken up, she had ranted and raved and he had just stood there, serene as the eye of a hurricane. And of course, she was the hurricane.

Evidently her movement caught his attention because he turned around. She tried to get her heart out of her throat, but she had to swallow several times before she succeeded. He studied her in a way that meant he really did want to talk.

Courtney started to come around the counter, but Jessica held up her hand and tried to give a smile of assurance. "Why don't you come back to the lounge, Austin? We can talk there."

Courtney opened her mouth as if to say something and then closed it. Out of the corner of her eye, Jessica saw Chad start to come forward, too, but she shook her head. He rocked on his feet as if he wanted to ignore her and come anyway, but he stayed, his arms crossed over his chest, his jaw firmly set. Marla looked back and forth between Chad and Jessica, eyes wide. Austin followed Jessica back to where she and Courtney had set up a reading area with a few second-hand couches and chairs.

She perched on the edge of one of the chairs, afraid to sit down on a sofa and have him come beside her. He sat on the chair across from her. She really didn't want him to start talking. After not seeing him for almost four months, it was hard not to drink in the sight of him. He didn't seem to have changed at all, but retained all the charming features that had attracted her to him in the first place.

His blond hair was combed perfectly to the right, and his green eyes were framed by gorgeous long lashes any girl would be jealous of. He clasped his perfectly manicured hands in front of him as he leaned forward.

"Jessica, you didn't answer my emails." He gave her a look a teacher would give an unruly student.

"I deleted them."

He lifted his chin. "I see you haven't forgiven me."

"I just didn't feel the need to let you back in my life." Jessica turned the wreath holder over in her hands.

"Did you at least read them?" Austin asked, and for the first time in her life, she heard a change in the tone of his voice. He sounded a little worried.

"I did." Jessica refused to say anything else yet. First, she wanted to see exactly what he wanted—where the conversation would go.

A customer wandered through the area, but didn't stick around to take advantage of the comfy furniture.

Austin waited for a minute, as if to see if Jessica would expound on her statement, but when she didn't, he said, "So, you know why I'm here."

"You mentioned you wanted to apologize." Jessica set the metal holder next to her so she would quit fiddling with it.

"And that you were right," he whispered, leaning in closer, "and I was wrong."

"Thank you for saying that." Jessica looked up and met his gaze. She used to love green eyes.

"I thought I could be a Christian and live like everyone else in the world," Austin said. Those words were what she had wanted him to admit months ago, but were they sincere now? He reached over and took Jessica's hands. His fingers around hers no longer felt like a perfect fit and she wanted to jerk away, but she also intended to remain much calmer during this conversation than she had at their last and didn't want to be rude. "When you pointed out that I couldn't, I got mad. But when I left that day, it was the biggest mistake of my life. Will you forgive me, Jessie?"

Jessica managed to pull her hands away. She really wanted to say "no," but knew deep down inside that she should forgive him. She had known it for weeks, really, but hadn't wanted to face it.

She saw movement out of the corner of her eye and turned to see Chad standing in the doorway. "You okay, Jessica?"

She nodded. "Fine."

He glanced between her and Austin. "Holler if you need anything."

"You think I'd hurt her?" Austin started to stand up.

"Austin ..." Jessica put her hand on his arm until he sat back down again.

"You hurt her once." Chad crossed his arms.

"Chad, stop." Jessica held her hand up. "I'll be out in just a minute."

He clenched his jaw and hesitated, then finally turned on his heel and walked back toward the front of the store. She waited until he left the room before she faced Austin again.

"Who is this Chad?" Austin stared at the doorway Chad had just vacated.

"Someone I've been seeing."

"You've already moved on?" Austin jerked his gaze back in her direction.

Jessica picked up the wreath hanger again and started playing with it. "Just for a month or so."

"Do you feel like I hurt you?"

"Austin, when we broke up, of course I was hurt." Jessica licked her lips. "Honestly, I had to talk myself into this new relationship because I was so scared ... I was scared that something like what happened with you would happen again. So, yes, I guess I was hurt. But I'm okay now."

"And you're moving on," Austin said almost to himself. He glanced back in the direction Chad had gone, as if to remind himself of reality.

"Yes."

He swallowed visibly and flexed his jaw. "So, this is it, then? Nothing else to say?"

"Austin, thanks for apologizing." Jessica paused, trying to figure out exactly how to say the next part. "I'm glad you changed your mind. But I'm pretty sure that's not the only problem we had in our relationship." She forced herself to look him full in the face. "I do forgive you."

Austin pointed back and forth between the two of them. "Just exactly what problems do you think we had?"

"I don't know." She shrugged, staring off toward the other side of the room. "I mean, when was the last time we had a real conversation? We started kissing and snuggling and everything so early in our relationship, I feel like that's all it became. In hindsight, I guess I led you to believe that I wanted you to ask me to move in with you, to take our relationship to an even more physical level. Perhaps, I should be asking your forgiveness."

"No." Austin tried to reach for her again, but she tucked her hands under her legs. "Jessie, no. That wasn't your fault. It was all mine. All of it was." He leaned even closer to her, his body barely remaining on the chair. "But I'm willing to change, to make sure we don't do that as much. I miss you." His eyes bore into hers. "I miss us."

Jessica looked away. Austin always had a charm about him, an ability to sound so sure of himself and what he was saying. Even now, he sounded so sincere. What was she doing, even listening to this anymore? She had Chad.

"All the physical stuff was a huge problem, but it wasn't the only one." She pointed to her chest. "I mean, how well do you really know me? Do you even know what one of my big goals in life is?"

"You want to write a book or something, right?" He shrugged. "I can totally support that. And like I said, I'm willing to change and learn more about you. I want to make this work."

Those emerald eyes held hers, pulling her, tugging on her heartstrings. The hurt in his gaze reminded her of a puppy dog. How could she send him away again without any hope? But wait a minute. This was exactly the look she gave her aunt or mom when trying to get her way, the one Chad had joked about using on Aunt Ruth before their family history had revealed its truth. She swallowed, regained some control. "I've moved on, Austin. Chad's a really great guy."

"But what if he's just a rebound? What if you're just dating him to get over our break-up?"

"Then, I guess I'll figure that out and move on again." But Chad didn't feel like a rebound.

"Well, I guess I'll go then. But if you decide that he is just a rebound, please, give me a call. I'll keep my number the same as long as I need to."

"Thanks, Austin, but ..." She shook her head.

He sat for another moment, as if he expected her to elaborate. When she didn't, he rose from his chair. She stood, too.

"I really was going to ask you to marry me," Austin said quietly. He walked out of the store and Jessica practically collapsed back into her chair. Was her heart still beating? She wasn't sure. Even though she hadn't been sure how she would forgive him, as she had said the words, she found them to be true. Austin had caused her quite a bit of grief, but her life was better now because of it.

Chad came in the room and sat where Austin had been. "My Mom is checking out right now."

Jessica looked up into his blue eyes and smiled. "I'm glad she found something."

"I just have one question: What is she supposed to think when she sees the girl I'm dating walk away with her ex-boyfriend?"

Jessica blinked. "We didn't go anywhere really private. Anyone could have walked in here. He wanted to apologize."

"And you probably forgave him."

"I did." Jessica tilted her head. "I think I had several weeks ago and just didn't realize it until today. He figured out that he was wrong."

"Are you sure he was sincere about it?"

"What are you talking about?" She frowned. "Why would he come here if he didn't really want to apologize?"

"Jess, I just think he's probably trying to manipulate you."

Manipulation? Into what? She wasn't going to change her mind on what she had told Austin all those months ago. "What would be the point?"

"You're an amazing girl." He stared straight at her. "I imagine he's just saying whatever he thinks will work to get you back."

"That's an awful thing to say!"

"I don't know. He just gives off this vibe ... like he's not completely honest."

"Well, he felt honest to me." Or did he? She wasn't even sure which way was up anymore.

Chad took a deep breath. "So where does that leave me?"

"What are you talking about?" Jessica frowned.

"You forgave him. Obviously, you were in love with him once upon a time. Is he back in the picture now?"

"No." Jessica emphatically shook her head. "We just tied up our loose ends and we're moving on with our lives."

"Really? Because it looked like you were holding hands with him earlier."

"He took my hands." Jessica rose and paced a few steps away. "I pulled them away again."

"I don't know." Chad motioned toward her as she walked past him. "The way you were looking at him." He studied her. "How do you explain that?"

"I don't even know what you're talking about." She threw her hands in the air. "I looked at him just like I look at anyone else." Sure. She still found Austin attractive, but she found Chad even more so. Couldn't he see that? "Why are you making such a big deal out of this?"

He stood, too. "Because you acted like you never wanted to see him again and then suddenly when he walks into your store, and Courtney tries to get him to leave, you invite him in to talk. It's like you're two different people."

"I'm the same person I was earlier this morning when you surprised me, the same one who spent the whole day with your family yesterday, the same one who likes smoothies and rode with you to Arkansas. I'm the one who got in a fight with my aunt over you. Remember me?"

"Yes, I remember that version of you. But do you want to be that person? I'm not even sure you know who you are or what you want. Because it looked to me like a part of you wanted to go back to being the person you were before you met me. Of course, even if you are the same girl I met, she allowed your aunt to cause you to doubt your feelings for me." Chad shoved his hands into the pockets of his jeans. "I'll tell you what. I'll do you a favor. I'm going to leave and give you time to figure it out."

She tried to catch his arm as he walked out of the room, but he shook her off. She followed him into the main part of the store, and watched him as he left with Marla.

Courtney glanced at Jessica in concern, but was waiting on a customer and couldn't help.

The bells jingled against the glass as the door shut behind Chad and his mother. How could she hear them over the sound of her heart breaking?

Chapter Nineteen

Things stayed fairly busy for the next week as people did their Christmas shopping. Every time Jessica went in and out of the store, she thought of Chad. The wreath he had brought was a beautiful circle of greenery with a huge red bow at the bottom. She added holiday decals to the windows and edged them with white lights. More white lights lined the counter and the banister, setting off a lovely contrast with the greenery. Ornaments hung from the chandelier in the reading lounge and from the tree she and Courtney had put in the entryway at the base of the stairs. The entire store exuded cheer, but it wasn't enough to lift Jessica out of her misery.

Even though she took turns at the cash register and stocking the shelves or helping customers, Chad stayed in the back of her mind. How had things gone so wrong? Wasn't she just sitting in a park with him discussing spending Christmas together and now he avoided eye contact across the auditorium at church? She blew a stray hair out of her face as she bent over a box in the back room and pulled out more children's books that were selling well. She grabbed three or four stuffed animals that were characters in the story and took them all out to the children's nook. Straightening some of the big pillows, she found a few books that had been left out and quickly returned them to shelves.

Carols played over the sound system, sending out messages of peace and joy. But Jessica couldn't find any. Courtney raised an eyebrow as Jessica walked back by the counter. Jessica tried to give her a smile that said she was okay.

It had been a week since she had spoken to Chad ... or seen Austin. She just wasn't sure what Chad thought she was supposed to be figuring out. Was he really mad about her forgiving Austin? True forgiveness didn't mean she had to bring Austin back into her life, right? No, she didn't have to try and make the amends Austin wanted. He might want her back, but she was where she needed to be with Chad. Why else would she fight with her aunt? She pushed back on the ache that grew inside her ever since Chad had walked out that door. Her heart had only fluttered at first sight of Austin that day because she hadn't seen him in so long. Yes. Maybe if Austin had suggested friendship ... she might have been open to that, but it probably wouldn't work considering their history.

"You're muttering to yourself again." Courtney bumped her playfully as she walked past the shelf Jessica was straightening.

"Sorry." Jessica leaned back on her heels. "I can't stop thinking about everything that happened last Friday. It's driving me crazy."

"Why don't you take the evening off? We've been working such long hours this last week that it's probably not helping. Go grab a bite to eat and then come back and help me close." Courtney tugged the paperback from Jessica's hand and helped her stand.

"Are you sure?"

"Yes. It's been rather slow today with the yucky weather. I'll call if I need you." Courtney gave her a quick hug. "Get out of here. Surely I can handle things alone for half an hour."

Jessica grabbed her jacket and purse and headed out to the smoothie shop. Needing something different, she ordered a pumpkin spice smoothie instead of the chocolate she usually got. The wind made it too chilly to sit on the patio like she normally did, so she claimed a table in a back corner of the restaurant. She leaned back against the chair and opened her book to read a chapter or two before she headed home again. After reading the same page three times, she put the book down on the table. The cover didn't even look familiar. What had she grabbed on the way out the door? Was this one of Courtney's books? She closed her eyes and took a deep breath. Her worries were getting out of control, taking over even the simplest of decisions.

"God, everything in my life seems so crazy right now. You know how I feel about Chad. You know I want to be his girlfriend and have a great relationship with him ... one like my parents and his parents have. Please help us to find a way to work through all these bumps we keep running into lately. Please, help me to finally be able to fully forgive Austin and let go of my anxiety over that situation. God, thank you for letting me be able to get out of that relationship without falling into the sin Austin wanted me to participate in."

She took a deep breath before finishing. "God, help me with my relationship with my aunt, too. I know she means well, but I can't let her be the only deciding factor in what I do regarding Chad. Help me to know which advice to take and which to ignore. And God, please help me to trust you more. Help me to put all these troubles into your hands and know that you will take care of them ... and in a much better way than I ever could."

The troubles and worries she had just prayed about floated up into God's large hands and He closed His fingers around them. When His hands opened again, the anxiety had vanished. With a little smile, she picked her book back up again. *Thank you, God.*

About a page into her novel—yes, it was her novel—she startled at a thump on the table in front of her. The scrapbook from Chad's grandfather's house lay there. She glanced up to see sad blue eyes.

"You said you forgave him." Chad looked uncertain. "Can you forgive me?"

She tossed her book in her bag, stood and hugged him for a long moment. He brushed the side of her hair with a gentle kiss and she closed her eyes to breathe in his familiar scent.

"I'm so sorry."

"I'm glad you're here. Austin's had me so confused." She leaned back to look at Chad. "Not confused in whether or not I should go back to dating him. But just trying to figure out what it really meant to forgive. When you reminded me the other day that he had been a big part of my life and that I had loved him at one time, it also brought to mind that as Christians we're supposed to love everyone, even people who have hurt us. I know I don't love him in the same way I fancied myself loving him a few months ago, but I do need to love him the way Christ loves us. And I'm not sure what all that means."

"Just because you're forgiving him and trying to love him like Christ, you don't have to let him back into your life. Forgiveness doesn't equal trust. He broke your trust and that's something not easily rebuilt." Chad squeezed her arms. "That guy didn't sit right with me for multiple reasons. Just the way he showed up out of the blue and was so insistent he talk to you … and how possessive he acted when I came around. It was obvious he was trying to get you back."

She pulled him to the table so he could sit in the chair beside hers. "But he left without much of a fight once he heard you were in the picture."

"Well, I hope for your sake that he is gone and willing to let you move on. I just have a feeling we haven't seen the last of him."

Jessica thought about Austin's parting words about not changing his phone number just in case she ever decided to take him back. Chad didn't need to know about that. "That doesn't mean I'm going to change my mind."

They sat for a few moments, just looking at each other. The silence wasn't uncomfortable. It was as if they were making up for all the time they'd missed spending together over the last week, a nonverbal conversation that spoke deeper than words.

"I have to admit. I might have been a little jealous of him." Chad caught her hands in his. "Okay. A lot jealous. And I was so mean to you."

She blinked in shock. "You were jealous? All week long I thought I had done something wrong. I mean, I don't think it was wrong to forgive Austin, but I kept going over in my head how I could have handled everything better. Was I wrong to not let you stay there with us? Was I wrong to talk to him then or should I have asked him to just let me email him back? All I wanted to do was tie up that part of my life so I could move on, and instead I feel like I just prolonged the agony somehow."

"No. Don't get me wrong. I was worried about you. But my mom pointed out that I was acting out of jealousy—I just didn't want to believe it. I've been fighting with myself all week over it. Even now. But deep down I know she was right."

"So your mom doesn't think badly of me?" Jessica held her breath for a moment as she waited for his answer.

"No. Are you kidding? If anything, she thinks badly of me."

She glanced down at the table and then back up at him. "I know this sounds bad, but I'm sort of glad."

"What? You're glad I got berated all the way home the other day like I was a nine-year-old again?"

"No!" She laughed. "I'm glad you were jealous. It's good for my ego." She gave a half-shrug. "And that I wasn't the only one miserable this week."

"I'm sorry you were miserable." He leaned forward and squeezed her hands. She wound her fingers through his long slender ones and enjoyed the security of the closeness. "I promised you that we'd make our relationship work no matter what happened in our families, but I guess I just wasn't expecting your ex-boyfriend to pop up again."

"I wasn't expecting him to show up again, either. But I promise," she said softly, "he's out of the picture. Especially if you're in it. I just have to wonder, though."

He raised one eyebrow in question.

"You've been telling me for several weeks now that I have to trust God, that it will be okay, and to remember that not all people are bad at heart. I know you think Austin was trying to manipulate me, but I can't believe he was truly bad at heart ... just wrong. But then it was like you couldn't trust me either. Isn't this supposed to be a two-way street?"

"Yes." He raked his hand through his hair. "I'm sorry I didn't take my own advice. We both need to learn from this, huh?"

"Definitely." She pointed heavenward. "I've been praying about our relationship lately. I really want it to work. And I've been praying that God will help me trust people more instead of just assuming everyone is out to get me."

"Maybe we should pray together." He gave a small smile.

"I'd like that."

"Me, too. I'm glad I didn't chase you right back into Austin's arms."

"I forgave him, and he admitted I was right, but I could never go back to him."

"Really?"

"I found something better." She looked up and met his gaze. "Honestly, if you hadn't shown up tonight, I was going to come to the clinic tomorrow on the excuse of needing cat food just to see if I could catch you there. And I still have half a bag at home."

He smiled and she returned his grin with one of her own. His stomach rumbled and they both laughed as the tension of the last week finally dissipated.

"Let me get something to eat. I'll be right back, okay?" He stood and she reluctantly let go of his hands.

Out of curiosity, she opened the black scrapbook and started turning the pages. Black and white photos were taped in, some with neat handwriting on the yellowed pages to let the observer know who was who in the pictures. Chad sat down next to her and leaned over to look as well.

"We never really got to go all the way through this before. I thought it might be fun to see if we could find some more pictures of our parents." Chad pointed to a picture of a little boy with curly hair wearing a sailor's suit. "That was my grandfather when he was a little boy."

Jessica turned the page and saw the same boy older with his arm around a pretty girl.

"My grandmother," Chad said around a bite of sandwich. "That was their wedding day."

"Isn't it funny how they didn't used to wear a fancy white gown as their wedding dress?" Jessica asked. "She had a beautiful new one, but I bet she wore it to church after that until it got all worn out."

They went on and saw the same couple with children.

Chad pointed to another picture. "My dad's brother, Andrew."

"I didn't know your dad had a brother."

Chad touched the photo solemnly.

"He doesn't anymore. Andy went to Vietnam and didn't come back." Chad set the remainder of his sandwich down. "I never met him. He died January of 1975."

Jessica turned another page to find the family had grown. Now there were pictures with the couple, Andrew, and two girls.

"My dad's sisters. That's Aunt Phyllis and that's Aunt Martha. Both of them are older than Dad. He's the baby."

"There he is." Jessica spotted the fourth child in a photograph on the next page with "Robert" scribbled underneath. As they continued flipping through pages, a distinct family resemblance could be seen, not only in Rob and Chad, but in all the men of the family. They all had the same wavy brown hair, and when the pictures had more color, she could see the same blue eyes.

"Here's a picture of Uncle Andy in his uniform right before he left." Chad pointed to a photo in the middle of the book. "He was going to Harding College. But I think he only made it through a year of school."

"What year?"

Chad silently counted, ticking years off on his fingers. "I think it was the fall of 1973 that he started there."

"I'm pretty sure that's the same year my aunt started there." Jessica tilted her head as she looked up at him.

"Small world." Chad popped the last bite into his mouth. "Do you think she knew him?"

"I have no idea." Jessica tilted her head. "Possibly. Why did he only make it through a year?"

"Evidently, he got so tired of hearing people complain about the war that he actually signed up to go to Vietnam. Dad always told me that story with a lot of pride in his voice."

They continued flipping through the book as they drank their smoothies.

Jessica gasped and grabbed Chad's wrist to look at his watch. "Shoot!" she exclaimed. "I told Courtney I'd be back in half an hour to help her with the store."

"When does it close?" Chad looked at the watch himself.

"In half an hour." She groaned. "I'm gonna owe her big time."

"Blame it on me." Chad shut the scrapbook and picked it up. Something fluttered to the floor.

Jessica leaned down and picked up the loose picture. On the back was a handwritten date: 1974. She turned it over and froze.

Chad leaned down to see what had caught her attention. He bent forward to get a closer look and then grabbed the photo out of her hand. Their eyes met in astonishment.

"I'd say your aunt knew my uncle," Chad finally said.

"I'd say so, too."

"Mind if I join you for Christmas? I want to see what she says when we show her this."

Jessica just nodded.

***

Jessica hurried back to the shop to help Courtney close up and then called her mother the next day to let her know she was coming for

Christmas. She piled books onto a cart to restock a few shelves of bestsellers while she cradled her cell phone between her cheek and her shoulder. She huffed as she stacked a few more books on top of the already mountainous heap.

"You okay?" her mom asked.

"I'm fine. Just moving books around while I talk to you."

"Well, I'm glad to hear you changed your mind about Christmas," her mom said. "Your aunt Ruth will be pleased, too."

Jessica paused before replying, "I wouldn't count on that just yet. Chad is coming with me."

"Jessica—"

"Mom, he's going to stay at his grandfather's house, but he and I both need to talk to her. And he gave me the same excuse I gave him when I went up with him a few months ago. He doesn't want me driving by myself."

Her mom sighed on the other end. "Please don't ruin the holidays for everyone by bringing up the past, Jess. Can't this wait until another time?"

"Mom, we think we may have figured out something." Jessica maneuvered the cart around a couple of kids who were running through the store to catch their parents at the cash register. "I'm not going to ruin the holidays. I'm going to try and find some peace with my aunt."

"I hope you know what you're doing."

"Me, too," Jessica said. "Me, too."

"We'll see you in a couple weeks then. And I'll try to help you figure out how to get Chad involved with the family festivities without making your aunt mad. But I make no promises."

"Thanks, Mom." Jessica slid three books onto one of the mystery shelves.

They ended their conversation and Jessica went to relieve Courtney at the counter. She had promised to cover the register for most of the day to make up for her extra-long disappearance last night. Courtney had seemed understanding, but Jessica didn't miss the look of relief on her face when she took over.

As Jessica checked people out, typing in their prices and bagging their new books, she had a lot of time to think. Ringing people up was a fairly mindless activity, so the photo stayed in the forefront of her thoughts. Chad had agreed to ask his dad if he knew anything about it, but he figured his dad would have mentioned it if he did.

Jessica wanted to know all sorts of things. Why was her aunt in a portrait with Chad's uncle? Why weren't there any other pictures? What were they doing all dressed up? Were they in love or just good friends? Was Aunt Ruth upset because he had died in the war or was there another reason? After all, dying in a war wouldn't make an entire family "no good" as her aunt continuously claimed. Right?

Why not just call her aunt and ask? But every time she went to pick up the phone, something inside made her stop. This conversation needed to be face-to-face. She just had to figure out how to start it.

And how to keep it from ruining the holidays.

Chapter Twenty

Three weeks later, Chad and Jessica loaded her little Toyota down with Christmas packages, suitcases, pillows, and homemade cookies. Chad shipped gifts to his family in case he didn't make it over to their side of Arkansas. Jessica couldn't imagine not seeing her family at Christmas, but she also dreaded the impending confrontation with her aunt. She wanted it over already, but knew she would have to wait until the perfect moment.

Courtney and Jessica had decided that they would shut down their shop from December twenty-third until January second. Their holiday sales had been better than expected and Courtney was going to travel with her parents to her grandparents' home in west Texas for Christmas. Chad assured Jessica that Lester would probably be okay if she just left a vacation feeder and water dispenser out for him, but she asked one of the girls at church to check on him and the mail while they were gone.

Jessica drove the first half of the trip, up through Dallas and east to Arkansas. Chad took over after a pit-stop between Dallas and Texarkana. Jessica leaned back in the passenger seat as the prairies passed her window. What few trees there were had mostly lost their leaves now and looked bare and lonely. She was glad for a break from driving as the Texas wind whipped against her car the whole morning.

"Have you figured out what you're going to say yet?" Chad asked.

"Not really. I also have no idea when I'm going to do it." Jessica pulled her feet up under her. "I want to uphold my promise to Mom and keep the peace and not ruin Christmas, but I also feel like I've waited forever to bring it up already because it needs to be face-to-face."

Chad nodded. "Do you think it would ease some of the tension if you just went ahead and brought it up when you first got there?"

"I think I'm going to sort of test the waters and see where I go from there. See if she really does welcome me when I walk into her house or if I'm going to have to tiptoe around her no matter what."

"I'll stay away for tonight. There's no need for me to make it worse by coming in right away." Chad glanced over at her as they entered Arkansas.

"What will you do tonight? I mean, besides sleep at your grandfather's house?"

"I don't know. I guess just hang out, go through some more things of his. I might run by the grocery store in the next town and make some extravagant meal for myself." He tapped his finger to the holiday song that jingled on the radio.

"I didn't know you could cook."

"I used to stand in the kitchen under my mom's elbows and watch how she did things. She would get aggravated at me every now and then, but for the most part, she talked me through things and I learned as I watched. I'm not sure I'd call myself a gourmet, but I can muddle through and whip things together that don't kill me when I eat them."

She laughed. "You're just full of hidden talents."

They stopped for a short lunch break in Texarkana. Just over three hours later, they passed the city limits sign for Sassafras. The holiday decorations were the same ones that had been out around the courthouse when she was growing up—giant lighted snowmen and a Santa with various candy canes and ornaments. They drove slowly through the small town, and he steered them easily onto her aunt's road without needing to be reminded of the directions. He pulled up in front of the two-story house and parked the car. Jessica took a deep breath as she looked up at it.

"It's going to be okay. It's your family." He reached over to grab one of her hands that were clenched in her lap.

"Mom and Dad aren't here yet. It's just Aunt Ruth right now." Jessica stared down at their intertwined fingers. "Maybe we should come back—"

"She invited you. She's not going to leave you out on the front porch until your parents get here."

"Are you sure?" Jessica wanted to believe him as the curtain moved in the front window.

"I'm sure." He gave her hand a squeeze. "Want to pray before you go in?"

He had started praying with her every night over the last few weeks and they were closer than ever. She nodded her agreement with his suggestion. He took her other hand and they both bowed their heads.

"God, we thank you for our safe travel," Chad prayed. "We now ask for you to be with us through this holiday as we spend time with family. We love them and they love us, but that doesn't always make it easy to get along, God. Please help Jessica as she faces her aunt who she thinks doesn't want her here. Give her the words she needs to keep the peace and to help Aunt Ruth to see that she's not making as bad a decision as she thinks. God, help me to be good enough for Jessica."

She squeezed his hands between hers.

"And God, watch over us when we get ready to go home next week. Thank you for loving us, God. In Jesus' name we pray, Amen."

Jessica looked up into his eyes. "You are good enough for me. Better than good enough."

He gave her a smile and glanced toward the house. "Think she'll let me help you carry things in?"

"Maybe." Jessica shrugged. "I guess if all else fails you can just help carry them to the porch and I'll take them the rest of the way."

He gave a nod and opened the door. She had been dating him long enough that she waited for him to open hers as well. Then, they both loaded down their arms with bags and packages. Her aunt opened the door as they walked up the front steps.

"I don't have a place for him to sleep here." She said "him" with disdain in her voice.

"He's not sleeping here, Aunt Ruth. Just dropping me off for now." Jessica motioned to the pile in his arms. "Can he help carry things in?"

Ruth stepped back to let them walk through the doorway.

Jessica led him upstairs to the room she always stayed in. This trip she would have to share it with her younger sister, Brittney. She set her things down on the bed that used to belong to her grandparents. She had been visiting this house her whole life, earlier when her grandparents were still alive and now when it was just Aunt Ruth, but this was the first time she didn't feel welcome. It almost made her sick. "The packages go downstairs under the tree." She motioned with her head as Chad followed her into the room.

"Lead the way."

They headed back down the stairs and into the living room. Aunt Ruth had the artificial tree loaded with lights and ornaments that had been in the family since Jessica's grandparents first got married. She tenderly fingered an ornament Aunt Ruth had helped her paint as a child. She could still remember Aunt Ruth's hands gently pressing hers around the ball so that her tiny handprints formed a snowflake. With Aunt Ruth not having any children of her own, Jessica and Brittney had always found a second mom in their aunt. This time, however, Aunt Ruth was acting more like a wicked stepmother.

Jessica carefully set her packages around the bottom of the tree and then accepted the ones from Chad's arms.

They walked back out the door under her aunt's strict surveillance to get the remaining things. It was little enough that Jessica could carry it herself. She glanced back up at the door to see Aunt Ruth still standing there and took the things Chad had in his arms.

"Guess I'll take it from here." She hooked one last gift bag over her fingers.

"Call me later." He tucked a strand of hair behind her ear. "Let me know when you want me to come over. I feel sort of guilty taking your car."

"I won't need it," she said, "and this way you won't have to wait for me to pick you up."

"Talk to you later, then."

She leaned into his arms as he gave her a hug. She didn't care that her aunt stood on the porch watching. She needed that bit of affection before he left her alone with Aunt Ruth.

The gravel crunched under the tires as he pulled out of the driveway. She watched the car until it turned out of sight down the road. Then, she shifted her load and walked into the house. Aunt Ruth closed the door behind her, but didn't stop to chat with her or give a hug of welcome like she would have in the past. She hoped that by the end of this trip she would be able to at least have a hug good-bye.

Jessica set the last few gifts under the tree. A quick scan of the gifts already there revealed at least one with her name on it. She had to smile. She hadn't been sure Aunt Ruth would get her something. She straightened and found her aunt standing in the door of the living room watching her.

"Are you going to flaunt your relationship with him the whole time you're here?" Aunt Ruth asked.

"That wasn't my purpose in giving him a hug good-bye." Jessica tried to keep her voice even. "I just felt sort of bad that he was going to have to spend the evening alone while I got to spend it with family."

"Maybe you shouldn't have invited him if you didn't want him to be alone tonight." Aunt Ruth folded her arms across her chest.

"Actually, it was his idea to come with me. Sort of a return of me coming with him a few months ago. And because he likes spending time with me."

"Humph. Well, your family probably won't be here for another hour or so."

"Want me to hide until they get here?"

Aunt Ruth shrugged and turned away. "I'm sure you'll do whatever you want to do, no matter what I want." She walked down the hallway to the kitchen.

Jessica sighed and climbed the stairs to her room. At least while she waited she could clean off Brittney's side of the bed. She moved her bags to the corner where they were out of the way and then lay across the bed with a book. She tried to focus on the problems of the couple in the story, but instead, her own crept continuously into her brain.

Her mother's friendly "Hello!" carried up the stairs over an hour later as her family came in the front door. Sounds of luggage rolling on the hardwood floors and her sister's laughter followed. Jessica put her book on the nightstand on her side of the bed and walked down the stairs. Her mom looked up in surprise from hugging Aunt Ruth.

"I didn't think you were here yet since your car wasn't in the drive." Her mom glanced back outside as if she had missed seeing it.

Jessica moved into her hug. "I let Chad take it for the night. I figured that way he wouldn't be stuck at his grandfather's house with nowhere to go."

"Hey, Jessie-bear." Her father wrapped her up into his big arms. "How's my girl?"

"Good, Dad. Thanks."

She hugged her sister next.

"Ha! I'm finally taller than you." Brittney ran her hand from the top of her head over Jessica's. It was only about an inch higher than Jessica's five foot one body.

"Come on, Brit. You should really aim for loftier goals than that." Their father laughed.

Jessica rolled her eyes and tugged a strand of Brittney's brown hair, long like their mom's. Their whole life, people had asked if they were twins, despite being three years apart in age. Fortunately, since Jessica had moved out and Brittney had gone to college the last couple of years, the girls got along much better than they had when they were in school. Jessica smiled in anticipation of late-night conversations with her sister over the next few days.

"How's senior year?" Jessica asked her sister.

"Ugh. Too many papers. I thought I was never going to get through last semester." Brittney set a purse on the table. "But now all that's left is student teaching."

"And staying out of trouble." Their father nudged Brittney. "No boys allowed. I'm not really sure I approve of your sister having a boyfriend."

"Dad, please. If you ever want grandchildren, you have to let us date boys first." Brittney wrinkled her nose. "Not that I've found one I'm interested in yet."

"Well, don't count on grandkids from me anytime soon. Chad and I are still getting to know each other." Jessica held up her hands.

"Is Chad's family coming to Sassafras for Christmas, too?" her mom asked.

Aunt Ruth's eyes shot daggers at her mom, but Jessica answered anyway. "No. He's here solely for me."

"So he's eating alone tonight?" Her mom put her purse down on the hall table.

"He said he'd be fine." Jessica gave a nod.

Having her family there as a buffer seemed to ease some of the awkwardness. They made it through dinner without any sniping comments from Aunt Ruth. And Jessica didn't taste any extra salt or anything strange in her meal, so her aunt must not be trying to poison her. As she played cards with her family that evening, though, she longed for wisdom of how to start the conversation that would take place in the next few days. Too bad Chad couldn't have joined them this evening.

Chapter Twenty-one

"Why don't you tell Chad to come over this afternoon?" Jessica's mom whispered to her the next morning. "We'll probably do our dinner tonight and open presents."

"What about Aunt Ruth?" Jessica leaned against the banister across from her mom.

"I'll deal with her."

Jessica went back to her room and pulled out her phone. "Hey."

"Hey." His voice sounded groggy. "How's it going?"

"Well, she hasn't kicked me out yet." Jessica absentmindedly rearranged the jewelry her sister had left strewn all over the dresser top. "And there haven't been any actual explosions, but there's definitely some tension in the air."

"I'm sorry."

"Did I wake you up?"

"No," he said. "Although I have been fairly lazy today."

"That sounds nice." Jessica plopped on the bed, crossed her legs, and fiddled with a loose thread on the quilt. "Want to come over this afternoon? Mom invited you. She said we're going to do Christmas presents and stuff this evening since we'll have church tomorrow."

"And your aunt?"

"Mom said she'd handle it."

"I'll come over after lunch, then."

"Okay." Jessica couldn't keep from smiling. "I'll see you then."

It was beginning to feel weird to not say, "I love you," at the end of a conversation with Chad. She smiled again at that thought even though it made her heart speed up. She stuck her phone in her pocket and headed back downstairs to curl up in front of a cheesy holiday movie with her dad.

When Chad rang the doorbell after lunch, Jessica ran to let him in. She threw open the door and stepped out onto the porch to give him a hug. He held a bag of gift boxes. Jessica pointed to the stash of presents and frowned.

"What?" He winked. "Isn't it Christmas?"

"I just didn't expect you to get anything for my family." Jessica shrugged.

"It's rude to show up at someone else's holiday celebration without gifts." He chucked her gently under her chin.

"C'mon, Jess. Don't keep him to yourself. We want to meet him." Brittney stuck her head out the door. "Especially after everything you told me about him last night."

Chad raised his eyebrows.

"It was nothing bad." Jessica stepped back from Chad and introduced him to her sister. "Chad, Brittney. Brittney, Chad."

He gave a wave and then followed them into the house. Brittney took the packages to place them under the tree and Jessica's parents moved into the entryway. Her dad shook Chad's hand as well, but her mom stopped and stared at him for a moment.

"I know Jess said you looked like your dad, but I really wasn't expecting it to be quite that much," Jessica's mom finally said with a small smile. "He definitely influenced your genes, didn't he?"

"Just like you influenced your daughter's." Chad lifted one of his shoulders. "I figure it could be worse. I could have taken after the dog."

Everyone laughed, and Jessica's dad slapped him on the back.

Chad followed her mom into the living room, holding onto Jessica's hand the whole way. The smell of turkey began to creep out of the kitchen where Aunt Ruth had sequestered herself when the doorbell rang. The clatter of the banging pots and pans rang down the hallway. Chad cast a cautious glance in that direction, but then sat down on the couch beside Jessica and her dad.

"So, Chad." Her dad turned the volume down on the television. "Jessica says you're a veterinarian."

"I am. I actually run my own clinic. I was blessed enough to inherit it from the man I interned under at the end of school."

"Where did you go to school?" Jessica's mom asked.

"I actually graduated from veterinary school at Texas A&M."

Jessica caught a glimpse of her aunt standing in the doorway, but she disappeared again before Jessica could invite her to join them.

"So, you moved to Texas because of school and not because your family is down there?" her mom asked.

"That's right." Chad crossed one leg over the other and leaned back, obviously more at ease with this interrogation than Jessica had been with her own at Thanksgiving. "My family is actually still in Arkansas, up near the Paragould area. Dad works with a Christian school up there as well as helping with a summer camp. And Mom is a CPA, so she can work anywhere."

Jessica watched her mom as she heard Chad talk about his dad, but her mom didn't show any sign of regret. Aunt Ruth didn't come around much that afternoon, but Jessica had a good idea that her aunt heard most of the conversation anyway. Hopefully Ruth would change her mind about how she treated Chad.

The family sat around the table for turkey, dressing, and mashed potatoes. The green beans were from Aunt Ruth's garden. Her dad led the family in a prayer and then everyone took a helping and passed the dishes to the left. Jessica loaded up her china plate. She grinned at Chad as she remembered the paper plates they had used at Thanksgiving. He smiled back and she knew he remembered, too.

"This is a really good turkey, Ruth." Jessica's mom motioned with her fork.

"Thanks." Aunt Ruth glanced up and then took another bite of mashed potatoes.

"So, I found out that one of the schools I get to student teach at is the same one where mom did her student teaching." Brittney took a sip of iced tea. "How cool is that? And I think someone said it's the same principal, believe it or not."

"I'm not that old, Brit." Jessica's mom smirked.

"Could someone pass the butter?" Chad looked down the table. The butter dish was right in front of Aunt Ruth, but she made no motion to pass it. After several awkward seconds ticked by, Jessica reached over and grabbed the dish herself.

Jessica's dad frowned at Aunt Ruth before focusing his attention on her. "So, Jess, how did your sales end up this year?"

Jessica swallowed a bite of stuffing. "Pretty good, actually. It was our best year yet, which gives us hope. The way eBooks are taking over the market, our store wasn't exactly a sure bet."

"If anyone can make it work, you girls can." He winked at her. "You always were my business-minded one."

"This dressing is your best yet, Aunt Ruth." Jessica forked another bite. "Someday I need to get the recipe from you."

"Hmm," was the only answer Aunt Ruth gave.

This was ridiculous! Jessica had to do something. Should she confront Aunt Ruth after the gifts were exchanged? She couldn't stand the thought of her aunt not talking to her the whole time she was there.

After dinner, she carried dishes into the kitchen. "Aunt Ruth, want me to help load the dishwasher?"

Her aunt remained silent as she rinsed gravy off a plate.

Jessica straightened and carried her dishes over to start putting them in the slots of the dishwasher. Aunt Ruth paused when she turned, but still didn't acknowledge Jessica in any other way before loading her own plates. Jessica blinked back some tears. Her aunt had always been blunt and straightforward with her nieces, but until now she had never been mean. Jessica finally stood right in the path her aunt was taking back to the dining room.

"I'm here, you know. Please at least acknowledge me."

Aunt Ruth focused on Jessica. "I know you're here. Trust me. I know you're here."

"What happened? We used to be really close. You were my favorite aunt, and I looked forward to seeing you every time we came here. I wanted to help you cook and go hit the antique shops and play dress up with your old clothes. Can't we be like that for at least a little while again? I'm still me."

Ruth tightened her jaw. Had she always had those little lines around her mouth? The worry wrinkles above her eyes?

Her mom leaned into the kitchen. "Are you two ready for gifts?"

Aunt Ruth continued to stare at Jessica for several seconds, her face full of emotions Jessica couldn't quite read. Finally, she swallowed and looked away. Jessica let out a breath she hadn't realized she had been holding and followed her mom into the living room. Chad frowned in concern as Jessica sat down beside him. He reached over and gave her fingers a squeeze.

Aunt Ruth perched in a wingchair across the room.

Brittney delegated herself the "elf" this year and began to pass out packages from under the tree. Jessica scooted to the floor in front of Chad to have more room. They each opened one at a time. Jessica carefully pulled back the paper from the corner of her gift from Aunt Ruth.

She removed a silver frame from the box. Staring back at her from behind the glass was herself, younger, along with Aunt Ruth and Brittney, all dressed up in fancy clothes. Jessica noted that her younger self had been wearing what she now knew was her mom's prom dress. Jessica ran her fingers over the picture as the memories of that rainy day came back to her.

"What is it?" Brittney scooted over to see.

"I didn't know you still had that dress." Her mom looked over Jessica's shoulder. "I figured Mama had gotten rid of it years ago."

"It's wonderful, Aunt Ruth," Jessica whispered.

Her aunt gave a slight nod.

More packages were opened. Paper was stuffed in a giant garbage bag, and piles stacked up beside everyone. Her parents gave Chad a new white coat with his name embroidered over the pocket.

"I guessed at your size by what your dad used to wear when he was a little younger than you." Her mom waved her hands in his direction.

"It's perfect." Chad slid it on to show it off.

"Looks good." Her dad gave a thumbs up.

"The dogs at the clinic will give me more respect now." Chad popped his collar.

Everyone laughed and even Aunt Ruth had to force her mouth back into a frown.

Brittney passed out the little square boxes Chad had brought to all the girls. "I've been dying to know what's in these." She gave hers a little shake.

"You all need to open them at the same time," Chad said. "Ready?"

Every woman gasped as they lifted the lids at the same time. Beautiful pearl earrings were nestled in cotton inside. The shape and color showed they were real. Jessica lifted them out to see them better.

"Chad, these are lovely." Jessica's mom fingered hers.

"Jessie, I like this boyfriend. He's a keeper!" Brittney slid her jewelry into her ears.

"I thought about earrings for you, too, but couldn't remember hearing if your ears were pierced or not." Chad handed her dad a long slender box and gave a teasing grin.

"Thanks." Her father chuckled and then opened the box and pulled out a silver fountain pen. "Nice."

Aunt Ruth pushed out of her chair. "Pie anyone?" Her box was still unopened on the floor.

As the rest of the family headed back to the kitchen, Jessica hung back with Chad. "They're beautiful, Chad."

"I'm glad you like them." He brushed a hair off her cheek. "The box for Aunt Ruth has another pair. That's why I wanted you to all open them together. They're all the same."

"I'm sorry she didn't even open it." Jessica glanced over to the box Aunt Ruth had left by her chair.

"Don't worry about it. They're hers whenever she's ready to accept them." He winked at her. "I have something else for you, too, but you'll have to wait until tomorrow for that. You've got to have something to open on Christmas day."

"I feel sort of guilty." She ducked her head. "I didn't get anything for your family. And you went all out for mine. And me, evidently."

"I enjoyed it." He squeezed her hand. "And my family won't expect you to have anything for them if we make it over there before heading back to Texas. I'm not worried about it."

"I still feel guilty."

"Well, don't." He playfully shook a finger at her. "Let's go get some pie. That will make you feel better."

She laughed and they walked down the hallway to the kitchen. As she pushed open the door, Aunt Ruth's voice carried over to them from across the room.

"All I know is that when I had a boyfriend at Christmastime, he didn't feel the need to buy off my family's affections with fancy gifts." Aunt Ruth turned with a slice of pumpkin pie in her hand.

Jessica started forward, about to retort that he had not been buying their affection, when Chad caught her arm and turned her to face him. She resisted, but he leaned forward and whispered in her ear, "It's not the right time. It's okay. Relax."

Taking a deep breath, she gave a slight nod and he loosened his grip. Throwing a glare over her shoulder at her aunt, she roughly pushed back through the swinging door, and stormed down the hallway and out the front door. The frosty air quickly cooled her heated face, and she paused, her breath coming out in a visible puff. She walked over to the glider bench and sat down on the frigid metal. It was the time of year when days were short and the sun was already gone, but the darkness of the corner of the porch matched her mood.

Chad came out with her jacket. "Thought you might need this."

She nodded, but didn't say anything. He wrapped it around her shoulders, and they rocked for a few minutes in silence. The wind blew a few flurries around in the evening air, only visible in the streetlight at the edge of the driveway. Jessica shrugged her coat on the rest of the way and zipped it up.

"You going to be okay?" Chad asked.

"Sure." Her voice held little conviction.

"We'll talk to her tomorrow afternoon, okay?" He pulled her cold hand into his and rubbed it between his long fingers to warm it up. "I've already told your mom we'll have our talk with Aunt Ruth after lunch. She thinks that's a good idea. She had no idea it was so bad."

Jessica nodded again. "So I just have to make it a little longer without snapping."

"You can do it." He gave her hands a squeeze.

"It's worth it, right?" She turned toward him.

"Right. Peace in the family is worth it. And it seems like maybe she needs to learn the lesson you and I have been learning the last couple months ... trust."

"I guess I'll just feel horrible if we go through all of this and then you and I don't work out. It will be like I put myself through almost ruining my relationship with my aunt for nothing."

"Thanks for your vote of confidence." He playfully bumped her shoulder with his arm. "Seriously, Jess. Do you really think we don't have a chance?"

"I guess I'm just nervous." She looked up into his eyes. "I'm just not sure how this conversation with her is going to go."

"Don't be nervous." He reached and stroked her cheek with the back of his hand. "It's worth it even if we don't make it—although it's my plan to make sure we do. If nothing else, you'll have helped your aunt get over whatever has gripped her in this sin for so many years."

"Sin?" Jessica asked.

"Isn't not forgiving a sin? Isn't that basically what you told me about you forgiving Austin?"

Jessica sighed and nodded.

"So for nothing else than that we're Christians, we need to do this. Tomorrow. After lunch."

"Tomorrow after lunch," she said.

"I'll go now, but I'll see you at church in the morning."

Jessica nibbled her bottom lip for a moment. "I really do like my earrings."

"Good." His blue eyes sparkled brightly enough she could see it even with only the streetlight to illuminate them.

"Did you get pie?" She let him pull her up with him as he stood.

"No, but I'll get a piece tomorrow. Your mom promised."

"Okay." Jessica smiled. "I'm sorry your night was ruined."

"It wasn't. I was with you all evening. My night was perfect." He brushed a kiss on the top of her hair. "Sweet dreams."

He drove away into the flurries. She shivered and pulled her jacket closer. That metal glider was almost colder than the air, and she had sat on it for about half an hour. She quietly opened the door and went back inside. She went straight upstairs without bothering to get a piece of pie for herself.

Brittney looked up as she came in the room. "Chad leave?"

"For tonight." Jessica perched on the edge of the bed.

"I like him, Jess. Even if Aunt Ruth doesn't see how great he is." Brittney folded a new sweater and set it aside.

"Thanks, Britt. Just pray for us."

"Of course." Brittney cleaned off the rest of her side of the bed and left to wash her face.

Jessica got ready for bed and slid under the covers, careful to stay on her side. Her mind wouldn't stop spinning. How would their conversation go with Aunt Ruth tomorrow? Would she even listen?

And, what else could Chad have gotten her for Christmas?

Chapter Twenty-two

Jessica looked up as Chad slid into the pew the next morning and sat beside her. She heard several whispers behind her, but chose to ignore them. These people were just going to have to get used to seeing a couple who reminded them of the past. She had decided the night before that her mom's past would not ruin Jessica's future.

Aunt Ruth sat at the other end of the row, with Jessica's parents between them. Her heart fluttered a bit as she thought about what would happen after lunch. Chad took her hand in his and tucked it into the crook of his arm and insisted that they share a songbook as worship services started.

The preacher pointed out that even though the world celebrated Jesus' birthday only on Christmas, as Christians, they should celebrate it every day of the year. Jessica reminded herself that Jesus had come to earth when He had probably wanted to stay in Heaven and had died so they could all have forgiveness of their sins. Then, she admonished herself that sin was one of the reasons they were going to sit and talk with Aunt Ruth that afternoon.

At the end of services, her mom leaned over to give Chad a formal invitation to lunch. Jessica decided to ride with him back to the house, even though they had all fit in her parents' car coming over. Aunt Ruth's face made her think that the ride would be more peaceful in her own car.

As they wove through the neighborhoods, Jessica's cell phone buzzed. She pulled it out and saw that she had a message. She read, "If you change your mind," and saw that Austin had sent her a picture. When it came up, she gasped.

Chad stole the phone out of her fingers. "Whoa. I had no idea this is what you wanted for Christmas. You should have told me."

Jessica leaned over and took the phone back. "Pay attention to the road, please. Besides, it's not what I wanted. It's what he thinks I want."

She pushed delete and the shiny diamond ring disappeared off of her phone. It wasn't as difficult as she had thought it would be. She put her phone back in her bag.

"I take it that was from Austin?" Chad asked.

"Yes." She licked her lips. "He told me the other day that if I had been willing to forgive and forget, he'd have asked me to marry him. I just didn't realize he was serious enough that he already bought the ring, too."

"Why didn't he ask you the other day?"

"You walked in and he found out I had moved on." She looked at Chad.

"Should I apologize?" He glanced over.

"No."

He peeked at her again as he parked the car in front of her aunt's house.

"I promise." She reached over and squeezed his hand. "You're the one I want to make things work with. Not him. Now, no more talk about my past." She looked up at the house and sighed. "We've got to go face Aunt Ruth's."

"Ready?" he asked.

"Ready or not," she said.

"Let's say a prayer first."

She nodded in agreement.

"God, you know what we face this afternoon. Jessica loves her aunt Ruth so much, but we can't understand why she is being so mean lately. Please help us to be able to get to the root of the problem so we can all regain peace. Help Jessica and me in our relationship. Help us to always trust you and please help us through the struggles of this life. And thank you, God, for this time with family and this avenue of prayer."

Jessica looked back up at the house. Her family had been going in when Chad pulled up and she knew she needed to join them. But she dreaded it, too.

"Maybe Mom was right. Maybe Christmas is a stupid time to try to do this. I'll just come back in a month or so ..."

"Jessica." Chad ran a finger down her cheek. "Can you really stand to have your aunt act like this for that much longer?"

The pain of everything that had happened over the last few months threatened to choke her. She shook her head and brushed away a tear. "No. Let's get this over with."

He opened the door for her and they walked up the front steps and in the house. The smell of ham and cheesy potatoes and baked beans filled the front hallway, along with Aunt Ruth's homemade rolls, one of Jessica's favorite memories. She breathed in deeply as she took her coat off and hung it on the coat tree. She was facing Aunt Ruth, not a monster. Aunt Ruth had been there for her forever. She could do this—would do this so that she could have her relationship with her aunt back again.

"Where is the picture?" Chad asked.

"Here." She slipped it out of her coat and moved it to his shirt pocket.

"Everything's going to be okay." He caught her hand and held it to his chest for a moment.

"It has to be."

"It will." He hugged her quickly. "We'll find a way to make things work no matter what. But let's hope for the best, okay? We just prayed about it. Let's trust God that He can help us turn this around."

She nodded. "Still working on that."

Chad held her hand as they walked in the kitchen.

"Can I help with anything?" he asked.

Aunt Ruth glanced over her shoulder, but then turned her back on them. Jessica's mom handed him a stack of plates and told him to go set the table. Jessica got glasses down and started putting ice in them.

In no time at all, lunch was ready and everyone sat down where they had been the night before. Her dad asked Chad to lead them in prayer as they all held hands around the table. Chad glanced at her aunt, but then nodded and bowed his head.

"Father God, thank you so much for this time to spend together with family. Thank you for your son and your forgiveness through him. Please watch over us as we continue to celebrate this holiday. Help our hearts to be kind to one another and help us to be like you, God. In Jesus' name we pray, amen."

He hadn't mentioned the food in his prayer, but it had covered much more important things than lunch. Everyone passed the laden platters and bowls and filled their plates.

It was the quietest Christmas dinner Jessica could ever remember, as if everyone waited with bated breath for the brewing storm to reach its climax. She didn't even know how much her dad and Brittney knew, but they must have sensed that something was about to happen. Brittney set her knife down harder than needed, and the clink had Jessica dropping her own fork. She bit her bottom lip and slowly exhaled.

Jessica took a bite of ham and met her mother's gaze across the table.

Her mom gave her a little nod like a silent promise that she would support her daughter no matter what happened this afternoon.

After lunch, Jessica and Brittney loaded the dishwasher and put away the leftovers. As Jessica scraped the few dabs of potatoes into a plastic container, she glanced over at her aunt. Aunt Ruth wrung out the dishcloth she had been using and continued cleaning her section of the kitchen. Jessica wasn't sure she could stand the strain much longer. Where was her mom? How much longer were they going to wait? Brittney gave Jessica a squeeze and then slipped away.

Murmurs sounded on the other side of the kitchen door. *Please let that be Mom and Chad. I can't take this much longer!*

Jessica's mom and Chad came in, both laughing as if they didn't even remember why they had decided to corner Aunt Ruth. They quieted down once they saw Jessica's face, and she could breathe easier simply because they were in the room now.

Chad met her eyes and pointed up to remind her who was in control.

God, help us.

Aunt Ruth had almost finished wiping down the counters when Jessica's mom and Chad pulled the chairs out around the kitchen table. Jessica's mom gently guided her aunt down in one chair and sat down beside her, holding her hand.

Jessica slid into the remaining seat, between Chad and Aunt Ruth.

"What's this about?" Aunt Ruth asked.

"Ruth, I let you ruin my relationship with Rob over thirty years ago." Jessica's mom glanced at Chad before she turned back to Aunt Ruth. "I don't mind as much now. I found Stan and I love him to death. But I shouldn't have let you be the one to decide whether or not I stayed with Rob."

Aunt Ruth opened her mouth like she was going to say something and then closed it again.

"It's not healthy that you're still holding on to whatever this grudge is you have against Rob and his family. I've never understood it, and I might not ever completely understand it. But I agree with the kids. We need to face this and deal with it finally."

"How dare you—"

Chad slipped the picture into Jessica's hand, and she pushed it across the table to her aunt.

Aunt Ruth looked down at the photo, glanced up at Jessica and then stared down again. Her fingers shook as she picked it up.

"Andy," she whispered.

~1973~

Ruth looked across her college Bible class at the boy making the point. The teacher led a discussion on something in Mark—she had lost track of exactly where they were. Instead, the tall chestnut-haired man standing to her right mesmerized her with his fiery blue eyes as he spoke.

She gathered her books after class and was about to stand up when she realized he was right beside her. She looked up into those blue eyes as a wave of heat crept across her cheeks.

"I'm Andrew Manning." He stuck out his hand. "I don't think I've met you before."

He was like no other boy she had ever known. After only a week of eating with him every day, she knew enough to know she liked him for more than just his looks. His goal was to meet everyone on campus before he graduated. One of his biggest passions was the war, even though it had just ended. He detested that people were boycotting it and still protesting it.

"Romans says, 'Let every soul be in subjection to the higher powers: for there is no power but of God; and the powers that be are ordained of God,'" Andy quoted as they sat across the table from each other. "These people who protest and cause all these problems for the vets coming back, they're not being Christ-like. They're not being subject to the government."

"Andy, they're just trying to let the government know that they don't approve of us being involved in the war." She speared a bite of tomato. "It's not even a conflict that really affected us, but we went over there to fight anyway."

"Yes, but our government made that decision. Even if we don't approve, we still have to honor it because we're supposed to honor the government since it's from God."

Ruth shook her head. "But what about all those lives that have been lost because of it? Doesn't that make it bad enough that it's okay for people to take issue with it?"

Andy leaned in closer, pointing to the table as if he were a preacher emphasizing a point in a sermon. "Further down in the same chapter in Romans, it says, 'He is a minister of God to thee for good. But if thou do that which is evil, be afraid; for he beareth not the sword in vain: for he is a minister of God, an avenger for wrath to him that doeth evil. Wherefore ye must needs be in subjection, not only because of the wrath, but also for conscience' sake.'" Pushing back, Andy leaned against his side of the booth. "God actually gives the government the authority to bear the sword, so to speak."

"Still railing against the injustices, Andy?" Another boy punched Andy's arm as he and some other friends walked by.

"Until they are no more!" Andy raised his fist in the air, bringing forth a rally call from the guys.

"You sure are passionate about all this." Ruth pushed aside a piece of lettuce that was past its prime. "You're not thinking about doing something crazy like volunteering to go over there are you?"

"I can't." Andy took a sip of his soda, a lock of his wavy hair falling across his eyes as he bent over.

She let out a breath she hadn't realized she'd been holding.

"Promised my folks I'd do a full year here before making any decisions about joining the Marines."

She was glad to hold him to it. They spent almost all of their free time together every day between classes and in the evenings. They compared childhoods: they were both the oldest, she had one sibling, and he had three.

"Surely you can't expect me to believe I had it that much easier just because I had fewer siblings." Ruth laughed as they walked to a basketball game together.

"Of course you had it easier. You only had one sister to lock in a closet for a moment of peace. I had two sisters and a brother to squeeze in there. Do you know how hard that was?"

She looked over at him, her mouth hanging open.

He threw back his head and his laughter echoed off the sides of the buildings they were walking between. "You should see your face right now."

"You didn't really lock your sisters and brother in a closet, right?"

"Just the oldest sister. And only once." He winked. "Mama warmed my backside so well that I knew better than to try it again."

Moments like this made her fall in love with him even more. Seeing his passion for Christ and his indignation about the injustice of the war showed her his serious side. But he had a way of joking that kept her on her toes, and a way of looking at life that made it seem less overwhelming.

"Let's just walk for a while. We've got a little time before curfew." Andy twined his fingers between hers as they meandered across campus after a devotional shortly before Christmas break.

"Sure." Any extra time she could spend with this man was definitely a good thing in her mind, especially as they were about to be apart for a month during the holidays.

"The moon sure is big tonight." He pulled her a bit closer, tucking his arm around her waist.

"It's almost like a spotlight, huh?"

"What if I don't want to be in the spotlight right now?" He grinned and pulled her over to a cluster of trees. "What if I prefer it just be the two of us for a little while?"

"I can't imagine you not wanting to be in the spotlight, Andy. Aren't you the one who said you wanted to meet everyone on campus?"

He rested against a tree and pulled her into his arms. "Not right now."

She placed her head on his chest and listened to his heartbeat drumming against her ear for a minute. "Don't let me forget to bring you your Christmas present before we leave on Friday."

"You didn't have to get me anything."
"I wanted to." She leaned back and looked up into those mesmerizing eyes. They reminded her of the Milky Way in this dim light. "You're very special to me."
"I'm not the kind of guy who gets gifts for people most of the time. It drives my mama crazy." He ran his fingers lightly over her cheeks. "But maybe I can come up with something that will help you remember me while we're apart."
"Hmm?" She leaned her face deeper into his hand.
He moved his hand and tilted her chin upward. Slowly, he lowered his head to hers. Just a breath before closing the distance, he paused, searched her eyes. She could barely breathe.
"I think I'm falling in love with you, Ruth." His breath came out in a puff that warmed her cold nose and smelled of the hot chocolate they had enjoyed earlier.
It was just as well that she couldn't speak. His lips closed the distance and pressed against hers, warm and soft. He lingered for several moments, though not nearly long enough for her. How could her heart beat so fast and not break in two? Slowly, her eyes fluttered open, reality returning.
"Do you think that might help you remember me?" He grinned.
"Possibly." She licked her lips. "You might have to try again just to be on the safe side."
He threw back his head and laughed. "Oh, Ruth. You're the best thing to ever happen to me."

"Oh, is that why you're laughing at me?" She pulled back and started to walk away, but he caught her hand.

"Come here, you." He dipped her back and planted a kiss on her as if they were the couple in the famous World War II picture.

He helped her straighten back up, and she muffled her laughter in his shoulder. After all, she wouldn't want someone to overhear her giggles and interrupt this perfect moment. Her first kiss. Magical.

"Is that what you wanted?" he whispered in her ear.

"It's the best Christmas present anyone ever gave me." She knew as they slowly made their way out of the grove of trees and back into the open, her heart was his forever, and she could never love anyone else ever again.

~1974~

Andy came back from winter break even more hyped up about the issues around the Vietnam veterans. The cold of the January evening kept most students holed up in the student center or the library if they wanted to socialize. The Front Lawn was fairly vacant except for the two of them, making it a perfect spot for him to jump on his favorite topic. "Just imagine if you had risked life and limb to go over and fight, wondering if you were going to get to come home to your loved ones, if you might have to suffer from guerrilla attacks or stepping on bamboo spikes you didn't see buried in the leaves as you walked. And then!" Andy hit his fist against the palm of his hand as his breath hit the cold air. It reminded her of smoke, accentuating his passion, and she had to force back a grin. "Then, you finally do get to come home and you don't get a parade or a welcome home party. No. Instead, people spit on you! *Spit*!"

Ruth knew better than to say anything when he got this riled up, and she most certainly didn't dare smile. He would cool himself down in a minute or so. She just waited patiently for him to get through his rant.

"I can't even imagine why anyone would think it was okay to spit on someone just for having been sent over to the war." Taking a deep breath, he shook his head and then as he released it, he looked over at her with a sheepish grin. "But you didn't deserve to have to listen to that. I know I'm a lot to put up with sometimes, but it just really aggravates me to see the way people behave about this." He came over and plopped down beside her.

She sat in a swing with him, not caring about the fact that at their Christian university, sitting in a swing with a boy led to rumors of engagement. "Andy, don't you think the government has it under control without your help?" She twined her fingers through his, enjoying the security in their strength.

"Why shouldn't I volunteer to serve my country?" he asked. "What makes me better than those men who just came back?" He faced her. "Why should I be safe when they aren't?"

"Why shouldn't you be? Isn't that what they were fighting for?" Ruth looked up into his sea-blue eyes.

"Ruth, it's not like it's going to be that dangerous now. A lot of people who sign up for the Marines never even go to battle. There's no assurance I would, either. But I feel like I need to do something." He raked his fingers through his hair, leaving several strands sticking up which made him that much more endearing.

"But if the war's over already, it's just a waste of time. I mean, you wouldn't even get to fight this battle you're so angry about, and then you'd end up stuck in the Marines for some thirty years." Ruth pulled her hand free and crossed her arms.

"What about all those souls over there still in danger or still recovering from all the fighting? Don't you think they need some Christians to come over and not only help them rebuild their country but also maybe get a chance to introduce them to Someone who can give them a better eternal life, too?"

She wanted to make a retort, but how could a person argue with someone who wanted to share the gospel?

"Ruthie, I wouldn't stop you from doing something you really believe in. Why are you so sure this is going to be so bad?"

Ruth decided to try a different approach. "What did your parents say when you told them?"

He sighed. "My mom cried, tried to talk me out of it like you're trying to do. Dad said I needed to finish this semester and do some more praying before I made such a big decision."

"And you should." She gave an emphatic nod. "It's a big decision."

"I know it's a big decision."

"But you're acting like it's not." She cringed at the whine she heard in her voice.

He reached over and cupped her cheek in his hand. "Ruth, I know it's a big decision. But it feels right to me. Don't worry. I'm still going to be praying about it over the next few months while I'm here. It's only January."

Chapter Twenty-three

~2011~

Jessica watched her aunt's face as emotions flew across it. Her mom reached over and held her aunt's hand. Chad had his arm around Jessica's chair.

"Where did you find this?" Aunt Ruth finally whispered.

"It was stuck in the back of a scrapbook we found in my grandfather's house. We were looking at pictures of my family and it slipped out. I knew it was my Uncle Andy, but it took us a few moments to figure out the girl in it was you." Chad gave a little shrug. "We wondered if it had anything to do with why you don't like my family."

Aunt Ruth took a deep breath. "I loved him." Her voice shook in a way that Jessica had never heard. "He was my only love."

It was so quiet in the kitchen that the tick of the clock seemed to reverberate in Jessica's ears as she waited for her aunt to say more.

Chad squeezed her shoulder.

Aunt Ruth stared at the picture, an almost haunted expression on her face.

"We met in college." Aunt Ruth shook her head. "He was only there a year."

"Where was this picture taken, Ruthie? I don't think I've ever seen it." Jessica's mom gently touched the edge of the photo, but did not try to remove it from her aunt's hands.

"It was the spring formal that the chorus had. Remember how I used to sing with the university chorus back then?" Aunt Ruth's hand fluttered around her collar. "He was my date."

There was another pause, and Jessica wondered if her aunt was reliving that night in her head.

"I thought maybe he was going to ask me to marry him that night." Her eyes grew moist. She blinked several times. "We'd only been dating since that fall, but we both knew that's what we wanted ... or so I thought."

"What happened instead?" her mom asked.

"He joined the Marines."

~1974~

"You did what?" She paused outside the doors to the formal dinner.

"You heard me, Ruth." He smiled at the other couples passing.

She pulled him over to a sitting area that was a little more out of the way. "And now I'm supposed to just go in there and pretend like everything's all right?" She stared, unseeing, at a piece of art on the wall, took a deep breath, swallowed a couple times, trying to control her anger and hurt. "I can't do that, Andy."

"You're being very dramatic. You knew this was coming. Why are you acting like this?"

"I kept hoping you would change your mind." She threw her hands in the air. "You hadn't brought it up in a while. That's really not the announcement I was expecting you to make tonight."

"Ruth, I'll still be your boyfriend, if you'll have me." He stepped closer to her and put his hands on her shoulders. "I still love you and I hope you still love me, too. But this is something I have to do."

Ruth bit her lips to keep them from trembling.

"You guys coming?" someone asked as they passed by and into the dining room.

"We'll be there in a minute," Andy said over his shoulder. He turned back to Ruth. "You going to be okay? We still have this night. And the rest of the semester, for that matter."

She took a deep breath and nodded. He took her elbow and escorted her into the room full of tables and chairs, decorated with fancy cloths and shiny dishes. The smells of beef, chicken, potatoes and vegetables wafted in the air amid the sounds of hundreds of chorus students chatting with their dates. The tablecloth tickled her knees as Andy helped push her chair under the table as they joined four other couples.

Ruth contributed very little to the conversation around them during the meal. She glanced over at Andy multiple times. She barely heard anything around her for the thoughts running rampant through her mind. Andy was right. How had she not expected this? But not so soon. She was supposed to have several more months to talk him out of this decision. Andy met her eyes and raised a brow, but she couldn't give him a grin to reassure him all was fine. Nothing was fine anymore.

"You two sure are quiet tonight." One of the boys broke through Ruth's musings.

Andy looked up and gave a solemn clearing of his throat. "I joined the Marines. I head to training right after the semester."

"I thought you said he was going to propose to you tonight," one of the girls whispered to Ruth, not quiet enough to be unheard by everyone else at the table.

Ruth's cheeks went hot as she glanced Andy's way and then back at the girl. She shook her head.

The girl must have realized her faux pas because she leaned back in her seat with a blush as well.

Ruth could feel Andy staring at her, but she focused on her roasted potatoes until she was sure he looked away. When she chanced a glance though, she met his blue eyes. She quickly studied her plate again. "I wonder what they're having for dessert?" She half-heartedly tried to change the subject.

The unhelpful whisperer touched her napkin to her lips, sending Ruth an apologetic grimace.

Several people looked her way, eyes annoyingly sympathetic.

Another girl took a drink and then giggled nervously as her glass clinked against the edge of her plate.

No one answered.

The rest of the dinner conversation became as bland as the potatoes had been. No one seemed to know what to say to get around the giant elephant Andy had loosed in the room.

Later, Andy stoically escorted Ruth to the car. He drove back to campus in silence. It was about an hour drive, and Ruth thought she was going to go crazy if he didn't say something before he dropped her off.

"I didn't tell her you were going to propose." Ruth finally broke the silence herself.

"Then, why did she think I was?"

"I mentioned you had an important announcement, and she obviously thought since we'd been dating all year—"

"I hate that." He sighed.

"What?"

"That just because you date a girl the whole school year, everyone on campus thinks you're overdue for an engagement. What's wrong with waiting until after school?"

Ruth didn't know what to say. She honestly didn't have a problem with that old-fashioned assumption. One of the reasons she had chosen to attend a Christian university was because she knew the odds of finding a Christian husband were better. She counted herself blessed when she had discovered the man she wanted to spend the rest of her life with her very first semester ... and now he was throwing it all away.

"Ruth, you know I love you. I've never loved another girl half as much as I do you. I'm just not ready to take that step yet," he said, pointing to his chest.

"Right," she whispered. "The Marines come first."

"You know that's not true. I'm going to love you even when I'm in the Marines. Every day I serve my country, I'm going to think of you. If you let me—"

"Andy, I'm never going to love anyone else but you. Of course I want you to still love me!"

"And we'll just pick up where we left off when I get back. It'll make our love stronger."

"Distance makes the heart grow fonder," she said. Her nose wrinkled as if she could smell the bitterness behind the sentiment.

"And if I were to the point of wanting to be engaged," he said, "I would definitely want to be engaged to you, Ruth Marie Anderson."

"I can't even imagine not seeing you every day." Tears welled in her eyes. She blinked, trying to force them back, but they betrayed her and slid down her cheeks.

"You have my picture. And I'll write you letters." He squeezed her hand.

They were back to campus now, and he maneuvered his car through the parking lot of her dorm to drop her off.

"It's not the same."

"No, it's not." He turned to her and cupped her face in his hands. "But it's going to fly by so fast you'll never even miss me."

She doubted that very much, but he was so sure, so she forced a smile.

~2011~

"This was in April and he left at the end of May for training." Aunt Ruth set the picture down. She got up and rummaged around in a drawer in the desk. From the very back, she pulled out a bundle of letters, yellowed with age and with a ribbon around them. She set them on the table in front of her and ran a finger over the top one.

"He wrote me twice a week while he was still training. He came to see me in November that year. I was still in school. He was about to head to Vietnam. It was just what he had signed up for. The war was over, but there were still people at the embassy in Saigon. He had a purpose in life. He felt he was doing the best thing he could by serving his country."

Jessica's mom reached over and held her aunt's hand.

Aunt Ruth sighed. "Before he left, he promised me ..." She paused for a long moment, but no one interrupted her thoughts. "He promised me he'd come back."

She didn't have to finish the statement. Chad and Jessica both knew that Andrew had died in Vietnam in April of 1975, at the very end of American involvement.

Chad gave Jessica's hand a squeeze as a tear slid down her cheek to mirror the ones on her aunt's.

"Ruthie, what happened?" Jessica's mom asked quietly.

"Uncle Andrew didn't make it back from Vietnam." Chad spoke up. "He was one of the few American casualties the day Saigon fell."

"The Marines pulled out at the end of the month, but it was too late." Aunt Ruth released a shaky breath.

Jessica listened to the clock ticking again. She could barely hear the television going in the living room where Brittney and her dad were watching another holiday movie.

Aunt Ruth cried quietly as her fingers mindlessly flipped the edges of the letters.

"Ruth." Jessica's mom looked confused. "I still don't understand. Why did you hate Rob so much?"

Slowly, Aunt Ruth looked up at her sister. "Don't you see?"

Jessica's mom shook her head.

Aunt Ruth dabbed at her eyes with a holly-patterned napkin. "Andy promised me he'd come back. He *promised*. And he broke his promise."

Her mom waited while Aunt Ruth cried. "Rob looked so much like Andy." Sniffling, she pointed at the picture. "They had the same eyes. Every time I saw him, I had to blink twice to confirm that it wasn't Andy. Same thing with Chad. All the men in that family have those blue eyes, that wavy brown hair."

Jessica still didn't understand, but she didn't say anything for fear her aunt would quit talking.

"If Andy would break a promise and break my heart, why wouldn't his brother do the same to you?"

Jessica glanced over and met Chad's blue eyes. They had found the root of the problem. Her aunt's heart was broken, and in her desire to protect the other girls from suffering the same fate, she had taken her caution to an unhealthy level. She had somehow convinced herself that it was Andy's fault that he didn't come back.

"Uncle Andy didn't go over there planning to die," Chad said quietly.

"He promised he'd come back." Ruth glared at him. "We were going to get married when he got back."

She pulled a chain out of her blouse. At the very end, a diamond ring dangled. An engagement ring.

"He was supposed to come back." Ruth's sobs shook her shoulders.

~November 1974~

"Ruth, say something." Andy knelt on the ground before her. "Stop staring at me with your mouth open and let me know if I'm going to get to be the happiest man in the world or not."

Ruth couldn't believe it. Here was what she had been hoping for and wanting for over a year. But it came at such a bad time.

"Andy, I'd love to marry you ..."

He leapt from the ground, picked her up and spun her around. "Oh, Ruth! I know this isn't the ideal, but you'll see. It's going to be great." He slipped the diamond on her finger and then brought her hand to his lips. "Perfect."

Ruth pulled away and stepped over to a bench at the edge of the park trail. Emotions flooded her heart. The chilly evening breeze stirred her hair and cooled her flushed cheeks. She studied the ring a moment before she spun to look back at her sweetheart. Her fiancé?

"But, Andy ... how on earth is this going to work? And what will my dad say? He's old fashioned. He isn't going to be happy that I'm engaged to someone he hasn't even met yet."

"We'll keep it between you and me for now. Just to give me a little extra something to look forward to when I come home." Andy came closer and took her hands again. "I ship out next week, you know."

"I know." It came out on a whisper as the thought choked her up. "I won't be able to stand thinking of you over there. I know the war is over, but I keep hearing how things are still so bad. Why couldn't they send you somewhere else?"

"They're sending me where I'm needed." He pressed her head against his chest. "God knows what He's doing. He's going to be with me there just as He is here."

Ruth closed her eyes and listened to his heartbeat. It was hard enough being at school with him several states away. How on earth was she supposed to survive having him across the ocean? She burrowed a little closer.

"Hey." He rubbed her back. "We can get through this. And just think how nice it will be to see each other when I get back. We'll have a whole stack of letters we can stash away for our kids to read some day. And I'll go ask your dad's permission like I should have in the first place. It'll be perfect."

"I guess I need to take this off for now, then." Ruth pulled away and looked at the ring again.

"I should have gotten you a chain or something." Andy squeezed her fingers. "Here." He yanked on the chain around his own neck, sliding his dog tags off. "I'm friends with the guy who issues these. He'll help me get another one hopefully before I get caught without them on. And it will suffice until I can send you something nicer."

The ring dangled against her chest as he reached around her neck and fastened the chain. She ran her fingers down the metal, still warm from his skin. It was the closest she would get to having a hug from him while he was gone.

"I love you, Ruth." Andy ran his finger down her cheek. "I wouldn't be doing this if I didn't. I'm not the kind of guy who steps into things lightly. You know that."

She nodded.

"We've survived the short time I've been in training. And we'll survive the short time I'll be over in Vietnam. We can't stay over there much longer, right? After all, peace was declared last year and the only troops still over there are just putting out the last few fires. You keep focusing on school and writing to me, and we'll be back together again before you know it."

"You'll be as careful as you can be, right? I don't want you dying in the jungles over there." Ruth clung to the ring and held his gaze.

"I'm going to come back to you." He kissed her gently. "I promise."

~2011~

"It's okay, Ruthie." Jessica's mom gently pulled Aunt Ruth over to lean on her shoulder and stroked her hair. "It's okay."

When Aunt Ruth had finally cried herself out, Jessica reached out and took her other hand. "Aunt Ruth, Rob and Chad aren't Andy."

Ruth nodded and sniffed. "I know."

"And even if they were, they'd still be great men." Jessica swiped at a tear that traced its way down her cheek. "Andy was a great man. He stood for something he cared about. But he also cared about you. And he wanted to marry you. He didn't mean to break his promise. It just happened."

Jessica's mom stood and grabbed a box of tissues from the other room. She passed the box to Aunt Ruth who passed it on to Jessica.

Jessica sought out Chad. Even his eyes were damp. His uncle had been the first Manning man to capture the attention of one of the girls in this family. Was there any way to fully mend the rift left because of Andy?

"I know you think he betrayed you by going over there, but he really did think he was coming back." Chad leaned forward, his elbows on the table. "I've read several of the letters he wrote to my grandparents. He was so excited to be serving his God and his country, but he also mentioned several times that he had something just as wonderful waiting back home. We just never knew what he was talking about until now."

Jessica looked sideways at her mom and exchanged a shaky smile.

"He kept telling me that in my letters, too." Aunt Ruth swiped at her nose. "Every one promised he would be back. Except one." She pulled one from the bottom of the bundle. "This is the only one I never read all the way through. I couldn't make it past the first paragraph."

The paper on this letter was more worn than the others appeared to be. It looked to have been wadded up and smoothed out again, and evidence of old tears smudged the words, but

Jessica accepted the correspondence with reverence, awed that her aunt would trust her with something so noticeably prized.

My dearest Ruth, if you're reading this ...

Jessica looked up. This was the final letter, the one Aunt Ruth should never have received.

... if you're reading this, you and Mama can both say, "I told you so." I know it's not what you want to hear. It's definitely not what I want you to have to find out, especially this way. This is the kind of letter most men write on one of their darkest nights, one when they're missing their families and their girl something fierce. Well, I'm definitely missing you. And while I hope you never have to read this letter, if you are reading it, please know that I never wanted you to have to miss me for that long, either. You shouldn't have to wait for Heaven to get your happily ever after.

Jessica quickly skimmed the rest of the page then glanced up at her aunt. "Listen to this, Aunt Ruth."

"'Sometimes, I think "What if I hadn't been so stubborn and decided to come over here despite what my parents and Ruth said?" It's definitely a different world from Arkansas. But not all of it has been bad. And I wouldn't really change my mind about coming. This was where I needed to be. Like Jeremiah the prophet, I had a "fire in my bones" that I couldn't quench. You see, it's been on my heart to become a missionary down the road. I thought, "What better way to see if I'm cut out for it than to see if I can teach a few people while I'm over here now?" I have a friend who is much better at speaking the native language than I am. He goes with me and we've been teaching a few people

English by using the Bible. Not only do they grasp more of our language than they had been able to pick up already, but they're also grasping the most important truth of all, that there is a God and He loves them.

"'So far, we've studied with fifteen men and twelve women. Ten have been baptized. More come each week. I know those numbers aren't terribly big, but just think about this. If I hadn't been over here, would any of them have heard the truth? Maybe. But I'm very happy that God chose to use me while I was here anyway.

"'Ruthie, I hope to tell you all of this in person. I hope you never have to read this letter. I'll burn it the day they tell me I'm coming home. But if you do have to read this letter, then I want you to know that I'm doing more than just serving my country. I'm serving our God, too. He gave me the fire, the anger I needed to have the desire to sign up to come. And then He put in me the words and ability to share His good news with the people over here. Because they have souls, too. And even though I'd rather be doing mission work with you by my side, I have to work while I'm able. I can't wait for the best moment. I have to serve in the moments I'm given.

"'God forbid you ever have to read this (I know I've said that all through this letter, but please know I really do mean it), but if you do, I want you to know how much I love you. Don't stop your life because of this. Don't let it hold you back. Let God use you in the moments He gives you. Selfishly, I ask that you keep a piece of my memory in your heart. But don't let it take up the whole place. You're a wonderful woman and you deserve to have someone love you like crazy.

"'May this missive never reach your hands, but if it does, know that I am and always will be, your Andy.'"

"I miss him," Aunt Ruth whispered.

"I know you think Uncle Andy went over there just because he was frustrated with the war protests." Chad shook his head. "I obviously never even knew him, but I heard stories. My grandpa used to tell me that, not only did Uncle Andy go over there to serve his country, he also went over there to teach the Bible. Evidently, when he was trying to convince my grandparents to let him sign up, the mission work was one of the reasons he gave them. It's why my grandfather finally conceded."

Ruth met his gaze for the first time since meeting him. Were they breaking through her hurt? What was going on inside her head?

Chapter Twenty-four

"Why didn't you ever tell me?" Jessica's mom leaned back in her chair. "I asked you so many times what you had against Rob's family and you always just said they would break my heart. No one ever knew why you were so set against them."

"I'm not completely sure." Ruth slipped her engagement ring on and off her finger, as if relishing the fact that she could finally admit to others its existence. "Maybe I was a little embarrassed. Maybe I was still too caught up in the grief."

"Embarrassed?" Jessica's mom asked.

"So many of my friends were engaged or married." Ruth looked up. "I had my degree, but no fiancé. And Andy had been there such a short time, most of my friends had actually forgotten I had even dated anyone. They couldn't understand why I wouldn't date anyone else, why I was so depressed all the time. And we hadn't even told our families we were engaged, so I couldn't just stand up at the

Christmas table and say, 'By the way, I met a boy and agreed to marry him, but he joined the Marines and died in Vietnam.'" Her voice was so deadpan no one could laugh, despite the absurdity of the mental image she had created.

"Papa never knew you were engaged?" Jessica couldn't imagine her grandfather approving one of his daughter's betrothals without the boy first asking his permission.

"There was no time for Andy to come meet him before he left." Ruth shook her head. "We were going to meet with him once Andy returned and then go do a quick ceremony somewhere before Andy would finish up school on the GI Bill. That was the plan." She gave a bitter chuckle and then slammed her hand down on the table. "Some plan."

Her ring hadn't been all the way on her finger and it flew off.

Aunt Ruth gasped as it skittered over the table and slid across the kitchen floor.

Jessica's heart skipped a beat as it got closer to the air vent.

Chad dove after it and cupped his hand over it before it could cause even more heartbreak. To everyone's great relief, he laid it in the middle of the table and sat back down.

Ruth reached like she might pull it back to her spot, but she folded her hands in her lap instead.

"And then when you came home, I was falling in love with Rob." Jessica's mom gave a wry smile.

"I knew his family was from Arkansas, but I never expected them to move to our town. I actually saw Rob before you did, at the grocery store he worked at. I was so glad no one was around that I knew because I just about passed out. I thought I was seeing Andy's ghost. I knew I had to keep you away from him."

"But I met him at that youth event at church." Jessica's mom stared at the other side of the kitchen as if she were watching a movie of their past on the front of the fridge.

"It was like seeing myself a few years before." Ruth nodded. "When you told me you were going to marry that boy, the one who looked so much like Andy, I couldn't help but think about how I had felt the same way about his older brother. And how I wasn't ever going to get the chance."

"I was so confused by you when you came back from college." Jessica's mom drew her attention back to her sister. "I knew you'd be different after being gone for four years, but you were more than just different. It was like you were a shell of who you had been before ... and not nearly as nice. You wouldn't ever talk to me except to snip and snarl."

"I didn't mean to be that way." Ruth tore a paper napkin into thin strips, piling them on the table in front of her. "It was just so hard. So hard to watch you actually getting what I could never have."

"I wonder what would have happened if you had told me all this back then."

Jessica cut a glance over at Chad. Would they have even existed? If Aunt Ruth had talked all this through back when Jessica's mom was dating Chad's dad, they might never have broken up. She got a little case of heebie-jeebies at the thought.

"I honestly didn't think you'd listen to me." Ruth rearranged the salt and pepper shakers on the lazy Susan in middle of the table, carefully placing them between her and the ring. "You were so stubborn."

"Right." Jessica's mom poked Ruth in the arm. "Because you aren't stubborn at all."

Ruth's grim expression cracked for a second as a smile tried to break through. "I suppose you're right. I haven't ever told anyone this, not in all these years."

"That can't have been easy." Jessica whispered. "I can't imagine keeping something like that inside." She reached over and clasped Chad's hand under the table.

"I guess I just figured it was my burden to bear. Your mom was so much younger than me. And she was just bound and determined to marry Rob." Ruth shook her head. "I couldn't stand it, and because of that, I ... well, I decided to try and break them up."

Jessica's mom reached over and touched Ruth's arm. "It makes more sense now that we know why. But Ruth, you did more than just try to break us up."

Ruth stilled her hands where she had been fidgeting with the mess of napkin pieces and looked at her sister.

"Ruth, you were downright vicious. Mean. Hateful." Jessica's mom leaned closer to her. "I wish I had confronted you years ago, been more relentless at trying to figure out why you were so against our relationship. Not so I could stay with Rob, but because I should have wanted to help you get over whatever demons were possessing you to behave in such a way."

Ruth frowned, smoothed an invisible wrinkle from her skirt. "Hateful? I only did what I felt I had to do to keep you from making a horrible mistake."

"You've got to be kidding me. Ruth, you said some absolutely callous things to both me and to Rob." Jessica's mom half stood and leaned over to look her sister squarely in the eye. "You're the reason he suggested we break up."

Ruth didn't even flinch. "I told you he would break your heart, Sandy."

"You really can't see it, can you? You really can't see past your own hurt to see the hurt you've caused others."

Jessica watched the back-and-forth between her mom and aunt, unsure how to help. This seemed all her fault. If she hadn't decided to confront Aunt Ruth in the first place, the sisters wouldn't be at odds with each other again. She glanced over at Chad to see if he had any suggestions, but he gave a slight shake of his head, as if to say she needed to let it play out.

"You've always said you were glad you ended up with Stan. I don't see why you're bringing all this up now anyway." Ruth flipped the picture of Andy and herself facedown. "All it did was bring up bad memories."

"Ruth." Jessica's mom sat again and took her sister's hands in her own. "Yes. I'm glad I ended up with Stan. But don't you see? I might have been happy with Rob, too. There's no one person in this world that's perfect for another. But if we truly love each other, we can make it work with whomever we choose to be with. I had chosen Rob, and we could have made it work ... except he didn't want to come between you and me. He said it was more important that I be able to work things out with you and regain a good relationship with my sister."

Ruth looked away.

"Don't get me wrong." Jessica's mom squeezed Ruth's arm. "I'm glad that you and I finally did work things out. And I'm glad my daughters have had you in their lives. But it wasn't fair of you to dictate how it all happened. And it isn't your right to tell Jessica who she can or can't date, either."

"Even if I know it will lead to heartache?" Ruth practically spat out the words.

"*You're* the reason Rob and I ended in heartache, Ruth. Not because of anything he did." Jessica's mom shook her head. "Think about this. What if we had our roles reversed? What if Andy hadn't died? But, what if I had dated Rob while Andy was away and had broken up with him? Then, if I saw you and Andy together after he came back, I decided that he was going to break your heart because his brother broke mine? What would you have done?"

"That's ridiculous."

"Exactly. It's ridiculous. Even if people are in the same family, it doesn't mean they're going to act the same. But that's what you did. You illogically assumed that just because something bad had happened in your relationship, something bad would happen in ours." Jessica's mom leaned back in her chair.

Ruth looked back and forth between Jessica and her mom. Jessica had always known her mom and aunt were sisters, but she'd never seen them fight like she and Brittney used to. This gave her a completely new perspective on their relationship.

"Ruth, we said it earlier and I'll say it again. It wasn't Andy's fault he died. I'm sorry it happened. I think I would have liked to meet him." Jessica's mom turned the picture back face up. "If you're going to judge the other men of his family, do it on his good merits. It sounds like that's what they all share along with their blue eyes."

Ruth ran her hand over Andy's face in the photograph. "He was the best man I ever met."

"Ruth, Chad isn't going to sign up to be a Marine. He isn't going off to fight a war," Jessica's mom said. "He's a veterinarian, and he has his own clinic there in Honey Springs. He's going to stick around and be there for Jessica."

"I suppose in my head, I know that." Ruth took a deep breath. "My heart has just been holding on to Andy for so long, to my disappointment with him, to my heartbreak ... I guess ... I just convinced myself that the rest of his family would break your hearts, too."

"I don't have any plans to break your niece's heart." Chad leaned forward, his forearms on the table.

"Maybe you'll be the first Manning to not break one of our hearts." Jessica's mom smiled and reached over to pat his hand.

"Is that even possible?" Aunt Ruth asked.

"Anything's possible." Jessica glanced over at Chad before grinning at her aunt. "Earlier today, I wasn't even sure you were ever going to speak to me again."

Ruth looked up, a stricken look on her face. "Oh, my sweet Jess. And I said all those ..." She lifted a hand and covered her mouth.

Jessica's mom leaned forward to catch Ruth's attention. "Ruth, listen to me. It's in the past. It's over."

"Why have you even been willing to talk to me all these years? After I acted like that."

"Because you're my sister. And I love you." Jessica's mom smiled.

Another round of tears slid down Ruth's cheeks. "All my pain. My hurt. I let it ruin your life."

"No."

"But you're right. You could have married Rob. Anyone could see you really did love each other. Even I could see it. I think that was why I was so bitter about it. I couldn't have that. But you could."

"No, Ruth. I promise. Stan has my heart completely. I will always love Rob, but I love Stan as a husband. I really think I was so desperate to marry Rob, in part, because you didn't want me to." Her mom looked sheepish at the admission.

Aunt Ruth opened her mouth in disbelief.

Her mom laughed. "It's not fun to have your older sister boss you around, especially when it comes to boyfriends."

The smile from a few moments before broke through this time, and a laugh burst from Ruth's lips. The other three joined in. With the laughter, the tension eased in the room.

Jessica let out a breath and released her death grip on Chad's hand.

Ruth leaned back in her chair and wiped the remaining moisture from her eyes. Even the sun shining through the window seemed a bit brighter.

Aunt Ruth would still have a long road ahead of her to truly get past her heartache and prejudice, but having things out in the open and admitting the possibility of having hurt those she loved was a good place to start. Jessica would take every bit she could get of the progress they had made this afternoon. Hopefully, true peace would come in the future. Aunt Ruth turned to Chad, looking down at the table. "I've been horrible to you."

"It's forgotten already." Chad gave her a grin.

Aunt Ruth cast him a humble smile, her gaze flickering to his. "Thank you." Aunt Ruth turned to Jessica. "Jessie ... "

Jessica rose and stepped over to her aunt to wrap her in a hug. "I love you, Aunt Ruth."

Chapter Twenty-five

It was chilly outside, but not too cold. Chad and Jessica bundled up in coats and scarves and gloves. He took her hand and they walked down the street to the park. The streetlights were just beginning to come on as were the Christmas lights on the homes they passed. One had an inflatable Santa on an inflatable motorcycle. Unfortunately, one of Santa's wheels was a bit low and he was flopping in the wind. Chad pointed it out and they both chuckled.

They stopped at the swings, and Jessica tried to forget the last time she had been there. The previous visit to the park down from Aunt Ruth's house had held tears, but this one held the promise of an ending as happy as those movies her sister and dad had watched all afternoon. She plopped down onto a swing and kicked her legs to start moving.

"The stars are coming out." Chad pointed to the sky as he sat next to her.

"They're so much easier to see here in Sassafras than back home in Honey Springs." Her gaze followed his.

"Less light pollution." His finger drew a line to the southwest. "There's Orion."

"And Cassiopeia."

"Which one is that?"

She pointed to five stars that looked like a sideways "w." "It's supposed to be her throne."

"I didn't know about that one." He tracked her slow back and forth motion for a moment before looking back at the stars. "Just the usual—the dippers, Orion."

"I think I learned Cassiopeia from a movie, sadly enough." She kicked her legs. "I don't usually go around and learn random constellations."

"Right."

They swung in silence for a while. The rest of the sunlight faded and the stars came into more complete clarity. Almost every house on the block now had lights on in their yard. Jessica pumped her legs a little less and rubbed her hands together to warm them up as the cold started creeping through the wool of her gloves.

Chad dragged his feet across the ground to halt his motion, then reached over and held the chain of her swing until she was still as well. He pulled a box from his pocket. "I'm surprised you haven't been hounding me for this."

She cautiously took it from his hands. "It's not a ring, is it?"

"I thought you said you didn't want a ring." He reached for the box, but she clutched it to her chest before he could.

"I don't. That's why I asked. I wanted to make sure you weren't trying to move that fast."

He caught her chin in his hand and gently turned her head to face him. "I promised I wouldn't."

"I know. Sorry. Guess I'm still working on my trust issues."

"It's not a ring." He got out of his swing and crouched in front of her. "It's just the rest of your Christmas gift. As I promised."

"Something to open on Christmas day." She repeated what he had said the day before to let him know she had been listening.

"Are you going to open it or just overanalyze it all night?" He leaned his elbow on his knee, grinning at her.

She gently lifted the lid to reveal a necklace to match the earrings he had already given her. One single pearl nestled in a setting of a silver loop and dangled from a delicate chain. She lifted it out so that it hung from her fingers and glowed in the moonlight.

"It's beautiful," she whispered.

"I'm glad you like it."

She reached out and squeezed his shoulder. "I love it. But now I feel even worse for not getting you much."

"Hmm. Let's see." He leaned back on his heels and pretended to think for a moment. "You didn't run screaming from me when I came up and made a move on you at the smoothie shop that first day I met you. You trusted me even when you barely knew me during the hayride. You came to Sassafras to go to my grandfather's funeral. You have had a crazy couple of months since then because of your aunt's history with my uncle."

She waved her hand dismissively.

"You put up with my family for Thanksgiving, even when my mom threw a fit about not having real plates. You turned down another guy—even when he sent you a picture of a huge diamond—for me."

She started to say something, but he put his fingers over her lips. "You allowed me to spend Christmas with you. You captured my heart and for some reason are letting me stay in your life. I can't think of anything else I'd want."

"Nothing?" she asked, breathless. Was he going to kiss her? Was she ready for that step?

Instead, he put his finger to his chin and rolled his eyes up toward the sky for a moment. Then, he shook his head. "Nope."

She swallowed a tinge of disappointment.

They walked slowly back to her aunt's house.

She glanced over at him. "Why *did* you stay through all of this?"

"What do you mean?" He cocked his head.

"I mean, you put up with all sorts of mean things from Aunt Ruth." She pointed to her chest. "I was a basket case. It brought out all sorts of awkwardness between your parents. But you kept coming back to me, no matter what."

"Something inside told me you were worth it." He gave her elbow a squeeze. "And I believed you when you said your aunt wasn't usually like this. You knew her best. You knew what she normally acted like, and if you said this wasn't normal, then I was willing to work through it. And things will take a while longer to really get her back there, but I think we made great headway today. Just having her actually admit the heart of the issue had to help the healing process a little, right?"

"I hope so." Jessica blew out a breath of air. "My mom said she's going to take some time off and come stay with Aunt Ruth for a while, see if she can keep her talking now that she's finally opened up. She said she has years and years of boy talk to make up for."

"Let me guess." Chad batted his eyes. "They're going to gush over my blue eyes."

"Evidently, we all have it bad for blue eyes. Aren't you glad you inherited them?" Jessica gave him a cheeky grin.

"Definitely," he whispered close to her ear, making her heart speed up again.

"So, we've solved all the problems, right?" She quickly returned the subject to where it had been. Something in the night air had her emotions running higher than usual. "Now that Aunt Ruth admitted what the actual root of the problem was."

"Of course." He grinned. "We'll never have another problem for the rest of our lives."

She laughed and pushed at his shoulder. "That's not what I meant and you know it."

"Jess—" He paused as they reached the porch. "Why are you worried about it? Even if we do have problems, that's something we can tackle when they come up ... not something to worry about now. If we worry about it now, we'll just have ulcers when they do happen, and that'll only make it worse."

She laughed again. "So, we'll work through problems as they come along."

"If all else fails, we'll just return to Smoothie Heaven and find each other again. We'll always have our love of smoothies."

"Even if yours have wheat germ in them." She wrinkled her nose.

He pulled her to stand in front of him. "All that matters is that we both like each other and both want to see where this relationship goes."

She licked her lips and whispered, "Love each other."

"What?" His eyes locked with hers, searching, a hint of joy shining through the sea of blue.

"You said we like each other. But I don't just like you, Chad. I love you."

He ran a finger down her cheek. "I love you, too. I just didn't want to scare you off by saying it."

"Really?"

"Would someone who didn't love you willingly go through half of what we've had to put up with over the last few months?" He gave her a smirk that showed he was teasing. "Yes, Jessica. I love you."

She licked her lips again.

He glanced at the porch ceiling and then back down at her. "What a shame."

She looked up. "What?"

"No mistletoe."

She fought back a smile. "Who needs mistletoe?"

"I promised you I wouldn't move any faster than you wanted me to," he said softly and brushed a strand of her hair back behind her ear.

"I already owe you at least two kisses," she whispered, "for Lester."

"I'll collect those later." He leaned in a bit closer. "This one is for us."

She nodded, holding her breath.

He cradled her face. It was really going to happen this time. Her heart sped up, and she lifted her face to him to show that she was ready. Gently, he brought his head down and touched his lips to hers, softly at first, and then more firmly. She wrapped her arms around his waist and wondered why she hadn't given in to this sooner.

As he stepped back, they both exhaled, sending a cloud into the cold air.

She swallowed and then smiled up at him.

"Think Aunt Ruth would still approve of me if she knew I was out on her front porch kissing her niece?" He brushed his thumb against her cheek.

"Something tells me she and Uncle Andy probably kissed a few times, too," Jessica replied with a smile.

"So, what comes now?"

"Hot chocolate?"

He laughed. "That sounds like a great start."

They went back into the house. Jessica showed off her necklace, and they all sat around the living room drinking cocoa. And as Jessica held Chad's hand, she was really glad she loved smoothies.

The End

CPSIA information can be obtained
at www.ICGtesting.com
Printed in the USA
LVHW11s0452250918
591251LV00001B/14/P